BANKING ON LOVE

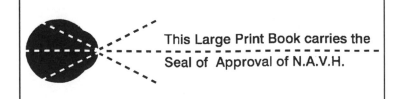

This Large Print Book carries the
Seal of Approval of N.A.V.H.

TEXAS WEDDINGS, BOOK 3

BANKING ON LOVE

A WOMAN SEEKS LOVE
THAT WILL ENDURE HARDSHIP

JANICE A. THOMPSON

THORNDIKE PRESS
A part of Gale, Cengage Learning

GALE
CENGAGE Learning™

Detroit • New York • San Francisco • New Haven, Conn • Waterville, Maine • London

GALE
CENGAGE Learning

LIBRARY OF CONGRESS CATALOGING-IN-PUBLICATION DATA

Thompson, Janice A.
    Banking on love : a woman seeks love that will endure hardship / by Janice A. Thompson.
        p. cm. — (Texan weddings ; bk. 3) (Thorndike Press large print Christian romance)
    ISBN-13: 978-1-4104-0859-4 (alk. paper)
    ISBN-10: 1-4104-0859-0 (alk. paper)
        1. Houston (Tex.) — Fiction. 2. Large type books. I. Title.
    PS3620.H6824B36 2008
    813'.6—dc22   2008014358

Published in 2008 by arrangement with Barbour Publishing, Inc.

DEDICATION

To all of my married daughters and their
  spouses:
Randi and Zach, Courtney and Brandon,
  Megan and Kevin.
The weddings are behind you, but the fun
  is just beginning!
I'm praying for Happily Ever Afters!

CHAPTER 1

Kellie Fisher pulled the keys from her purse and sprinted across the parking garage in search of her new sports car. "I was on level 2." She looked around, confused. "Right? Or was that yesterday?" Her days, filled from morning to night with work, seemed to run together into a dizzying haze. She could hardly remember her own name, let alone where she had parked the car.

She glanced at her watch and groaned. 6:47 p.m. In exactly thirteen minutes, in an exquisite downtown hotel ballroom, her husband would be honored for his work at Siefert and Collins, one of the busiest oil and gas accounting firms in the state of Texas. He would deliver a speech she had helped him craft. And she would miss it if even the slightest thing went wrong. Finding the car was critical to her survival.

She took the elevator to the next level and located the vehicle at once. The stunning silver sports car gleamed — a gem among the oceans of cars in the parking garage. Still, it was little consolation for her tardiness. "Please, Lord," she prayed aloud as she climbed inside, "please don't let there be any traffic. Just this once."

The new car started with ease, and Kellie made her way through the traffic in the parking garage, hands gripping the steering wheel. As she pulled out onto Westheimer, one of Houston's busiest streets, a mob of cars greeted her. Horns honked. Drivers shouted. An officer, face etched with frustration, directed traffic at the corner.

Kellie slapped herself in the head. "Not tonight. I can't be late. I just can't." If she missed even a minute of tonight's event, she would have a hard time forgiving herself. *I can't let Nathan down. I just can't.*

Then again, maybe she could use this time wisely. Kellie glanced in the rearview mirror. Her short blond hair needed a good brushing, and her cheeks, usually tanned and healthy, looked as if they hadn't seen the light of day in months. *I'll have to get to the tanning salon. Soon.* In the meantime, a little blush would have to do.

She stuck her hand in her purse and fished around for the small hairbrush. Once found, she pulled it out and ran it through her hair.

She opened a tiny silver compact and swept soft rosy blush along each cheekbone. "There. Much better."

A whistle blew several times, and Kellie realized she'd been holding up traffic. She shot forward a few short feet, waving her apology at the police officer.

"It's not as if we're really making progress," she grumbled. "And it's not as if I'm going to get there by seven either."

In the three years since she and Nathan had been married, Kellie rarely made it to an event on time. Her reputation for being fashionably late irritated Nathan, but what could she do about it? After taking on the job at Walsh and Weston, Houston's largest full-service brokerage firm, she'd scarcely had time to breathe, let alone eat or spend quality time with her husband. Her emotions ran up and down with the stock market, the highs and lows nearly taking her captive at times.

"We'll have more time together once things settle down." She spoke the words aloud to reassure herself, as always. In the meantime, she and Nathan would continue to build bank accounts, develop portfolios, and elevate their status on the job.

"Everything in its time." And time was critical, especially now.

She took a quick left onto a backstreet and wound her way through an upscale neighborhood, shooting for the short street that would empty into the west end of downtown. Kellie looked at the homes in awe as she sailed past them. Someday she and Nathan would own a house like one of these. They would sell their condominium and move up. When the children came.

"Everything in its time." She repeated the words again and glanced at the clock. 6:57. Three minutes. She focused on the road and forged ahead. She was grateful traffic seemed to be of little issue now.

Kellie allowed her thoughts to ramble a bit. She offered up a scattered prayer for Nathan, knowing his nerves were probably a jumbled mess as he prepared to face the crowd to speak. He always seemed to struggle with recognition and notoriety. As they had worked together on his speech late into the night, she could sense his edginess and slight embarrassment.

"You'd better get used to it," she had encouraged. "By the time all is said and done, you're going to be CEO. You'll be giving lots of speeches."

He responded with a shy smile and a slight shrug. "You'd better be praying a lot then."

"I am."

And she did pray for him. Every day, in fact. As she traveled back and forth to work, Kellie offered up words of thanks for the awesome man the Lord had dropped in her lap more than three years earlier while living in the Dallas area. At the time they'd met, Nathan had been engaged to someone else.

But God . . .

The Lord clearly had other plans. After the most lavish wedding anyone in the state of Texas had ever witnessed, the Lord had shifted Kellie and Nathan into a joyous honeymoon season. The years since had been spent in pure marital bliss. He'd opened doors for them to move back to Houston, prepared the way for her job at Walsh and Weston, and ultimately swung wide the doors for Nathan to move up quickly at Siefert and Collins.

Kellie was extremely proud of her husband's accomplishments, especially his ever-growing desire to help the underdogs he encountered along the way. She saw his commitment to the firm — and to her — and thanked God they had found one another.

With a prayer of thanks on her lips, Kellie pulled up to the hotel's valet parking area at 7:09. She checked her appearance in the

11

rearview mirror one last time. She applied a dab of soft pink gloss and climbed from the car. She tossed the keys to the attendant with a quick thank-you.

"You're welcome." He tipped his cap in her direction, then gave a whistle as his gaze fell on the car. "Wow. She's a beauty."

"Thanks." Kellie pressed her way through the crowd at the front door of the hotel and entered the grand foyer. Opulent light fixtures hung from the lofty ceiling, and expensive artwork framed the walls. For a moment she nearly let herself get lost in the splendor of it all. Until she remembered her purpose in being there.

Where is the ballroom again? Ah yes. Up the escalator and to the left. Or is it right?

She made it to the escalator in record time but managed to step aboard after an elderly couple, who stood their ground on the step above her. She glanced at her watch again — 7:11. Surely the banquet would start late. These things rarely began on time.

At the top of the escalator Kellie glanced to her left. Through the open doors to the ballroom, she could see her husband seated on-stage next to his boss. His lopsided sandy blond curls appeared a little more controlled than usual, but his long, gangly legs jutted out in front of the chair. No hiding that tall, thin physique. Kellie smiled in his direction. Nathan's stunning gray-blue eyes met hers as she entered the room.

"Sorry I'm late." She mouthed the words as she took her seat at the table nearest the stage.

Nathan shrugged and flashed a grin.

"At least he's not mad." Had she really spoken those words aloud?

"Kellie, it's nice to see you."

Kellie started as she heard her mother-in-law's words. For the first time, she realized she was not alone at the table. "Well, hello to you, too." She reached to give the older woman a soft kiss on the cheek.

"Glad you could make it." Nathan's mother smiled and turned her attention back to the stage. Kellie tried not to read too much into her words. *Did she think I wouldn't come, or is she scolding me for arriving late?*

Kellie's father-in-law reached to squeeze her hand and gave her a wink. She responded by gripping his hand tighter. Then, with nerves a bit frazzled, she leaned back in her chair and focused on her husband.

Nathan sat at his appointed place on the stage, twisting his cloth napkin in nervous anticipation as his boss made the necessary introductions. Truth be told, he didn't like it when people bragged about his accomplishments. It was hard to hear and even harder to talk about.

And yet, that's exactly what he must do. Tonight Nathan must stand before a roomful of his peers and discuss his achievements in the world of oil and gas accounting. That's what they expected. Why else would the firm have chosen to honor him as their Man of the Year? Why else would the bigwigs from Dallas have come down to Houston to share in his moment of glory?

Nathan looked out to the front table, where Kellie sat with his parents. *Lord, she's beautiful — inside and out. I don't know what I ever did to deserve her.* On the other hand, he didn't know what he would do without her. They were truly one flesh, sharing common interests, common goals, and common likes and dislikes. Not every couple could say that, and he didn't take it for granted. He hoped he never would.

I'm not sure when I've ever seen two people more jointly fit. That's what the pastor had spoken over them on their wedding day. And time proved him right. Kellie was Nathan's equal in every way. In some ways her head for knowledge and ability to play the role of chameleon when necessary gave her an added edge over him. She seemed to be moving up at the brokerage house almost as quickly as he stepped up the ladder at the firm.

Nathan snapped back to attention as his boss, Marvin Abernathy, turned to face him and loudly proclaimed, "Please welcome Nathan Fisher — a man with a head for numbers and a heart for the people. He's one of the hardest workers I've ever met, and he's our Man of the Year at Siefert and Collins."

Beads of sweat popped out on Nathan's brow. He wiped at them with the back of his hand, willing the lights overhead to dim.

As he stood and took the first step toward the podium, Kellie erupted in applause. Nathan threw a "Please don't do that — you're embarrassing me" look, but it did no good. She stood to her feet and clapped with great gusto. Others in the crowd followed her lead, and by the time he reached the podium, the whole place was on its feet.

"Congratulations, Nathan." Mr. Abernathy extended his hand. Nathan shook it warmly and then reached into his pocket for the speech he and Kellie had written together.

His hands shook, and he tried to still them as he spoke. "Thank you all." He looked over the crowd as they took their seats once again. "I can't thank you enough for being here tonight. It's an honor and a privilege to work for a company like Siefert and Collins, and an even greater honor to stand before you — my friends and peers — tonight."

His hands continued to vibrate as he reached to unfold his notes. *Lord, please help me through this. You know how nervous I get.*

His gaze fell on Kellie, who smiled broadly and gave him a thumbs-up sign. Her encouragement and support, as always, motivated him. With Kellie on his side, he could do anything.

He muddled forward into his speech, spending a few moments talking about his transition from Dallas to Houston, then diving into the many changes he had brought to the firm. None of the things he mentioned was fabricated or at all exaggerated. He had accomplished a lot over the past several months. With the Lord's help, of course. But listening to everything laid out in such a succinct, practical way now floored him, perhaps more than anyone else. It did seem a bit overwhelming that the Lord had blessed him so much.

By the time he finished his speech, Nathan's armpits were a soggy mess. Droplets of water slid down the sides of his face, and his throat felt constricted by his collar. As he moved across the stage to take his seat, he fought the feeling that he might be sick. Still, in spite of the obvious struggles, he felt a small sense of satisfaction.

He looked out at Kellie, who dabbed at her eyes with a cloth napkin. She blew him a kiss, and he winked in her direction. In a few moments, when this nonsense came to an end, he would take her in his arms and kiss away those tears — even if they were tears of joy.

CHAPTER 2

Nathan mulled over the pastor's words as he and Kellie left the sanctuary of the large metropolitan church. *Relationships are like gardens. They need tending. Leave them to themselves, and they'll be overgrown with weeds in no time.* Nathan contemplated the words as he made his way through the crowd.

He looked over at his gorgeous wife. *Lord, I know I've been busy. I can't seem to avoid it. But I also know things are changing in my relationship with Kellie. Even when we're together, we're not really — together.*

They reached the spacious foyer hand in hand and stopped for a breather as the crowd thinned. "Where do you want to go for lunch?" Kellie tucked a loose blond hair behind her ear and looked up at him with those crystal clear blue eyes of hers.

"I heard some people in Sunday school mention that new Italian place on the interstate. We could go with them. That might be fun."

"I don't know." With a Sunday school class of one hundred plus, there could be a potential mob scene if they all showed up at the same place. Besides, he had been looking forward to some alone time with Kellie. And it wasn't as if they'd had much time to develop friendships with others in the class. They were too busy. In other words, they wouldn't be missed.

"What were you thinking? I'm totally open."

"Hmm." An idea struck. "I was thinking that new deli. They're close, they have good food, and we can be in and out in less than an hour."

"Good point." She gave him a suspicious look. "Do you have to work this afternoon?"

Nathan drew in a deep breath, knowing how many things needed to be taken care of today. "We'll see. I'm hoping for some downtime."

"Me, too." She nuzzled against his arm. "Sounds good."

"Just a quick lunch then." He smiled. "And maybe the afternoon will be kind to us." *Maybe there will be enough hours to accomplish everything and still spend some quality time together.*

They chatted all the way across the parking lot as they searched for the car among the other vehicles. One of these days, they'd arrive at just the right time and get a good spot. Today wasn't that day.

Kellie's eyes lit up as she spoke. "Since we're alone, I guess I should tell you something."

"Really? What's that?"

"I've wanted to talk to you about our financial portfolio," she explained. "I have quite a few ideas for diversification."

"I'm always open to new ideas," he agreed. "As long as the payoff is good."

"Not good." Her eyebrows elevated playfully. "Great."

"Speaking of great, I have some great news about one of my newer accounts. It's doing really well." He dove off into a lengthy explanation but stopped himself midsentence when he realized what he'd done. *I'm talking about work. Again.*

They both grew silent at the same time.

Kellie broke the silence with a soft chuckle. "We're a mess, aren't we? We don't know how to talk about anything but work." She climbed into the driver's seat of her sports car, and Nathan took the passenger seat.

"Sure we do," he argued. "We talk about

all sorts of things." All related to the future, of course. In his heart, he had to admit the truth. They rarely talked about what they were thinking, feeling, hoping in the here and now. More often than not, he and Kellie talked about 401(k)s and stock options. They discussed the possibility of one day selling their newly renovated condo in favor of a brick home. They talked about the what-ifs of one day having a child, where that child would attend school, and what sort of day care options might be most viable during the formative preschool years.

What they did not talk about, however, was today. But right here, right now, he would change that. "I'm starved." He grinned in her direction. "I'm going to order the biggest sandwich they have."

"I love their salad bar."

They plunged into a lengthy discussion about the benefits of adding fiber to their diets, which led to a discussion about staying fit, which in turn led to an intense discussion about the recent stock surge among fitness centers on the West Coast.

At some point along the way, Nathan stopped for a belly laugh. They couldn't seem to win for losing.

"Catch!" Kellie tossed the keys in Nathan's

direction with a smile.

He caught them and gave her a curious look. "Is this your way of saying you want me to drive your new car?"

"If you don't mind." She pulled her cell phone from her purse. "I need to call my mom. She left three messages this week, and I haven't had time to get back with her." Something about her mother's messages left an uneasy feeling, one she couldn't explain. At any rate, she would feel better after talking to her. Her mind would be eased and her conscience relieved of the guilt she now carried — guilt over being too busy to stay in touch with the people she loved the most.

"No problem." Nathan clicked the doors open and climbed inside.

"Whatever happened to the days when you opened the door for me?" She scooted into the passenger seat, punching numbers into her phone.

"Huh?"

"You used to —" *Ah, never mind.* She wasn't one of those girlie girls who needed a man to open doors for her anyway. And Nathan was far too busy — and too distracted — to remember a little thing like opening the door for her.

She finished entering the number, and the phone rang once, twice, three times — and finally shifted to the answering machine.

"Great," she mumbled. "It's the machine."

"You've reached the Conways." She recognized her father's cheery, south Texas drawl. "We're not here right now. Probably out back tending to the animals or up at the church singing in the choir. Leave us a message, and we'll get back with you."

"Daddy." She spoke with conviction. "Daddy, this is Kellie. I'm calling Mom back. She actually called me a couple of times this week, but I've been swamped with work. Tell her I'm free this afternoon if she wants to give me a call. I love you both."

Kellie clicked the phone closed and leaned back against the seat.

"Not home?" Nathan put the car into gear and pulled out of the parking lot.

"Guess not." She shrugged. "I'm a little worried. According to my mom's latest message, my dad hasn't been himself lately. Lots of headaches, that sort of thing." She closed her eyes and realized she had a headache coming on, too.

"Probably the change in weather." Nathan shifted gears and headed toward home. "Allergies always get to me, too. Springtime is the worst."

"Still . . ." Kellie drew in a deep breath and rubbed at her aching neck. "It isn't like

23

her not to be home on a Sunday afternoon. They're pretty settled into their routines."

"Just like us." Nathan reached over to squeeze her hand.

Kellie shot him a hopeful smile. "I hope you're not saying you've decided to spend this afternoon working after all."

"Well . . ."

"Nathan. It's Sunday. Even the Lord took one day off."

"I know, Kellie." He focused on the road. "It won't take long, but I have some figures to go over. If I want to make partner this year . . ."

"I know, I know." She bit her lip and fought to keep from saying more. "It's fine."

She could probably get some work done, as well. But that's not how she wanted to spend the day. She wanted to spend it cuddling with her husband. Watching a movie. Eating ice cream.

"Everything okay?" He looked her way as he shifted gears once more.

"Uh-huh. Just lost in my thoughts."

"I know things are crazy right now, Kellie." He squeezed her hand again. "But we're going to have so many chances to make up for it. Someday. We'll take that trip to Europe. Just the two of us. We'll find the perfect spot to renew our wedding vows.

Just name the place and I'm there."

"Austria." The word slipped out before she had time to analyze his proposition. She paused, thinking. "No. Germany?"

"Any place you like." He nodded in her direction as he headed onto the interstate. "This will be your trip — the vacation of a lifetime. Whatever you want to do, we'll do."

"A boat ride down the Rhine? Touring ancient castles?" She smiled, remembering the television travel show that had triggered such lofty dreams.

"We'll do it all," he spoke with assurance. "And we'll stay in the best hotels, too."

Kellie shrugged. "I don't care about that. It might be as much fun to find some quaint bed-and-breakfasts along the way. I don't always need the best of everything, honey."

He shrugged. "Agreed. But I want to give you the best. Anything wrong with that?" His cell phone rang, and he took the call.

"No. Nothing wrong with that." Kellie muttered the words, then slipped off into her thoughts for the rest of the trip. By the time they arrived at the condominium, she felt as if she could fall asleep the moment her head hit the pillow. They took the elevator up to the seventh floor, while she yawned the whole way.

Nathan opened the door to their condominium, and she stepped inside. No matter how sleepy, the sheer magnificence and beauty of this place captivated her. Granite countertops, recently installed, gleamed. Brand-new stainless steel appliances looked right at home sitting alongside them. Wood floors, special ordered, beckoned.

But Kellie had only one thing on her mind. She wanted — no, she needed — to spend time with her husband. Nothing else mattered right now.

"I know you have to work, but" — she put her arms around him and rested her head against his chest — "I thought maybe we could —"

His cell phone went off again before she could finish her sentence. He answered it, and she marched into the bedroom to change.

Once there, she slipped into a worn nightshirt she had owned since high school and climbed into bed. She turned on the television, hoping for an old movie, something romantic. She settled on an old episode of *The Andy Griffith Show.* At least it was in black-and-white.

Kellie had dozed off when the bedside phone rang out, startling her. She answered it with the most "awake" voice she could muster. "Hello?"

"Is that my Kellie?"

"Mama?" She sat up immediately, plumping the pillows to her satisfaction.

"How are you, baby?"

She leaned back against the pillows and yawned. "Sleepy right now. But good. How are you? How's Dad?"

"I'm doing pretty well," her mother responded. "But Daddy's still not feeling very well. The headaches are getting worse."

"You should take him to see Dr. Baker." Kellie tried to sound firm. "There must be some reason for them."

"We have an appointment for tomorrow morning, honey, so don't worry. I'm sure everything will be fine." She paused a moment, and Kellie noticed a change in her voice. "Now tell me, how are you and Nathan?"

"We're fine." Kellie sighed as she looked across the bed.

"You sound tired."

"We're both so busy —" Kellie changed gears, opting to keep her private life private. No need worrying her mother unnecessarily, especially not on a day like today, when her father wasn't feeling well.

"Do you think you'll have time to slip away for a visit anytime soon? I'd love to see you, and you know how hard it is for

Daddy and me to make that drive now. He's not much for getting out on the freeways anymore. I'm not either, to be honest. And the whole city of Houston is looking more like one big freeway every day."

Kellie could sense the seriousness in her mother's voice and responded as best she could. "You're right about that. And the construction is quite a challenge, too." She tried to sound encouraging. "We'll come soon. I promise."

"Thatta girl." She could hear the smile in her mother's voice. "Greenvine's not that far away. Just an hour and a half. Lots of people drive that far to get to work in the city."

"I can't imagine it." Kellie shook her head. "I'm glad I live so close to the office. I don't know how people commute."

"I don't either, but folks seem to do it." She paused. "I keep forgetting to tell you that several of your friends from high school have been asking about you. Did I tell you Julia is pregnant?"

"Again?" Kellie flinched upon hearing her former best friend's name. "Wow. How old is her little girl? Just a little more than a year, right?"

"Yes."

"Pretty close together, I'd say."

"Some people do it that way."

Kellie calculated her words before speaking. "And some choose to wait until they can afford to give their children a good life."

Her mother laughed. "Some folks would be waiting forever then. I'm glad your daddy and I didn't wait till the money came rolling in. You and Katie probably wouldn't have been born at all."

Kellie looked up as Nathan entered the bedroom. He pulled off his tie and slipped out of his shoes. He glanced in the mirror above the dresser, then raked his fingers through his sandy, lopsided curls. Then he turned to face Kellie with a wink and a pout.

"I need to let you go, Mom." Kellie smiled back at him, understanding his wink. "But call me tomorrow after you get back from the doctor's office, okay?"

"I will, baby. But don't worry. God's in control."

"Yes, He is. But call me anyway."

They ended their call, and Kellie looked up in time to see Nathan ease into the spot next to her. She nuzzled into his arm and planted tiny kisses on his cheek. "I thought you had to work," she whispered.

He smiled gently and traced her cheek with his finger. "Everyone needs a day off."

She was glad they could enjoy the rest of it together.

CHAPTER 3

When the phone rang in the middle of the night, Kellie's heart raced. She shot a glance at the clock. 2:53 a.m.

"Who is it?" Nathan's voice, groggy and confused, spoke out of the darkness.

"I can't see the caller ID. Hang on." She rubbed at her eyes and snatched the portable phone from its base as she recognized her mother's cell phone number.

"Hello?"

"Kellie?" Her mother's frightened voice greeted her. "It's Mom."

"Mom." She sat up in the bed and turned on the lamp. "What's happened?"

"Your daddy" — her mother's voice broke — "he's —"

Kellie's heart twisted.

"We–we're at the hospital. They've taken him for a CT scan. Or maybe they said an MRI. I — I can't remember."

"I don't understand." Kellie tried to order

her thoughts. Still half asleep, she struggled to comprehend her mother's breathless words. "Is it because of the headaches?"

"Yes. He felt much worse this evening, so he took some ibuprofen and went to bed around eight thirty. I was working on a craft project for the children's program at church. I should have checked on him sooner." Her mother began to sob in earnest now. "I feel so — so b–bad."

"What happened, Mom?" Kellie's heart pounded against her chest wall. *Dear Lord, please . . . please . . .*

"I crawled into bed around eleven thirty and tried to wake him. I wanted to see if he felt better. But he wouldn't respond." Her mother's words were rushed, emotional. "I couldn't wake him up. He wouldn't budge."

"Oh, Mom." Kellie leaped from the bed, phone still clutched in her hand. She reached into a dresser drawer and pulled out a pair of jeans. She pressed the phone between her shoulder and her ear and began to shimmy into them.

"At first I thought he was just sleeping. You know what a sound sleeper he is."

"Yes." Her father had always had the uncanny ability to fall asleep anywhere and everywhere — and to sleep through anything, including thunderstorms.

Her mother's voice choked again. "B–but he wasn't just asleep. At some point I knew we were dealing with something much more than that. That's when I called 911."

"What are the doctors saying?"

"They're not sure. Maybe a stroke. Or an aneurysm."

"Oh no." Kellie fastened her jeans.

"What are you doing?" Nathan crawled out from under the covers and gave her an odd look. "What's happened?"

"It's my dad." She mouthed the words so her mother wouldn't hear. "He's in the hospital."

Nathan flew into action.

"Mom," Kellie said with as much determination as she could muster, "Nathan and I are coming."

"Oh, honey. I'd be so — so grateful." Her mother's sobs intensified.

Kellie made her way into the bathroom and reached for her toothbrush. "Where are you?" She smeared toothpaste over the bristles.

"At the hospital in Brenham."

"Brenham?" She nearly dropped the toothbrush. "Why is he there? He needs to be here — in Houston at the medical center. We've got the best doctors, the best technology."

"Honey, we were in too much of a hurry. The paramedics wanted to get him to the closest facility, and Brenham was the logical choice."

"But —" Kellie stopped herself before entering into an unnecessary argument. They could always arrange to have him transferred later — with her mother's co-operation. "We'll be leaving here in just a few minutes. We can probably be there by" — she glanced at the clock again and saw that it was three — "by 4:45, I'd say."

"Just come in through the emergency room."

"I will. And I love you, Mom. Give Dad a kiss from me. Nathan and I will get there as quick as we can."

"Promise me you'll drive carefully. And pray, honey."

"I am already." As she hung up the phone, Kellie burst into tears.

Nathan wrapped her in his arms. "It's going to be okay," he whispered as he stroked her hair.

"I don't know. . . ." She stood frozen for a moment, then stepped away and brushed her teeth with fervor. When she finished, she turned to Nathan. "We have to hurry. I want to get there as fast as I can."

"Well, you can't go in that." Nathan

34

pointed to her outfit, and she suddenly realized she still wore her nightshirt over her jeans.

"Oh. Good point." She slipped on a blouse and pulled another one from the closet to take with her. *Just in case.*

"I hate to bring this up, but didn't you say you had a meeting at work this morning?"

Kellie stopped dead in her tracks and tried to focus. "Oh. Yes, I do. It's with a new investor. Great opportunity. Could be a lot of money involved — for him and the firm. And ultimately for you and me."

"What will you do?"

Kellie sighed. "I'll pass him off to Bernie." She hated to lose the opportunity, but this was significantly more important. "It's not as if he's alone anyway. We have a couple of trainees on our floor. They'll do whatever he asks."

"That's good."

"What about you? Anything critical happening at the office today?"

He pursed his lips. "I think I can manage, as long as I call by seven and let them know. I can always take my laptop, and I'll keep my cell phone handy."

"Me, too." Kellie felt guilty talking about such things when her father lay in a hospital bed in an uncertain condition, but what could they do?

Within minutes, she and Nathan were on the road, headed west on Highway 290. With her nerves a shaky mess, she felt better that he had automatically taken the wheel. He seemed to be calmer, cooler. She looked at him as they traveled along, new thoughts ripping at her emotions. Her feelings for her father were strong, but a guilty conscience tore at her as other thoughts emerged.

Lord, what would I do if something like this happened to Nathan? I love him so much. I couldn't make it without him.

She pushed desperate thoughts from her mind and turned to him for comfort. "Nathan?"

"What, baby?"

"Could we pray together?"

"Of course." He began to pray aloud, and her nerves calmed almost immediately. When he finished, she picked up where he left off, offering an impassioned plea for her father's health and safety. They finished the prayer, and Nathan reached to snap on some music.

"I'm thinking praise and worship music would be good right about now." He adjusted the stereo to play a new CD.

As he fumbled with the knobs, the words from one of Kellie's favorite scripture verses came to mind. *" 'I have told you these things, so that in me you may have peace. In this world you will have trouble. But take heart! I have overcome the world.' "* That verse from the Gospel of John had carried her through more than one tragedy. With God's help this mountain could be tossed into the sea, as well.

A familiar worship song kicked in, and she leaned back against the seat in an attempt to relax. Somewhere between the words of the scripture, the lyrics of the song, and her husband's hand squeezed tightly in her own, hope took root.

Nathan paced the halls of the small hospital, praying silently. In the hours since arriving, he and Kellie had taken turns consoling her mother and speaking with the doctors. From what he could gather, his father-in-law's prognosis was grim at best. He frowned as he relived the doctor's words: *Ruptured aneurysm in the brain. Immediate surgery to reduce bleeding and swelling. Medically induced coma. Chances of survival — less than fifty percent. Recovery time undetermined. Possibly weeks or months.*

Without a miracle he might not make it.

Nathan continued to pace, his thoughts churning. He was plagued with unanswered questions. If Kenton survived, would he ever be the same again? Would he have to relearn how to speak, how to walk? Would he be able to return to work? *Lord, I don't understand. How do these things happen? Kenton loves his work. And the people of Greenvine love him.* They also needed him. Kenton's work as city comptroller had garnered him the respect and appreciation of friends and neighbors. How would they manage without him?

"Nathan?"

He started at his wife's beckoning. "What, baby?" He looked up into Kellie's tearstained eyes, then opened his arms to her.

She leaned her head on his shoulder. "What will happen if he doesn't get better?" she whispered. "What will my mama do? What will I do?"

Nathan couldn't muster up the words to respond. And Kellie's question raised other troubling thoughts. *Lord, what would I do if anything ever happened to Kellie?* He didn't have answers, at least not yet. But one thing was for sure: He had to devote more time to her and less time to work. He had to let her know she took precedence over his job.

38

And he must start now.

"This is the first time I've ever had to face the possibility that I could lose someone I love." Kellie continued to speak in hushed tones. "It's scary." She paused for a moment. "I mean, I know God's in control, and I know for sure where my father would be, but still . . ." Tears filled her eyes. "I would miss him so much."

"Let's don't think like that." Nathan sat up straight in his chair, determined to put a more positive spin on the situation. "We're going to keep praying and speaking words of faith over him when we go in there. I've heard that people in comas can still respond to our words."

"I've heard that, too." Kellie's eyes reflected hope. She bit her lip, then looked at him squarely. "I have an idea."

"What's that?"

"I have my portable CD player in the car. And I have tons of worship CDs. Maybe they'd let me play some music when we go in to see him. I know Daddy loves worship music. And hymns. I've got that great new collection of classic hymns my sister recorded. He loves that one." Her eyes lit up for the first time since they'd arrived.

"Great idea." Nathan squeezed her hand. "And we'll pray every time we go in. Out loud. He'll hear us — I know he will. And even if his body doesn't respond, his spirit will."

Nathan drew Kellie to him and kissed her on the head.

"I'm so proud of you," she said.

"Why?" He looked down at her in vague curiosity.

"You're such a man of faith. Sometimes I feel so . . . inadequate. When the rubber meets the road, my faith flies right out the window."

If only she knew how weak I feel. "No, it doesn't." He kissed her on the forehead. "You have more faith than almost anyone I know. You just need time to adjust to all of this."

Her cell phone rang out, startling them both.

Nathan looked at his watch. 7:53 a.m. "Who's calling this early?"

"It's Caroline from the office," Kellie explained, looking at the caller ID. "I'm sure she only wants to check up on things."

Kellie took the call, and Nathan's thoughts wandered as her conversation shifted. He could tell she wrestled with the need to be in two places at once. He understood that dilemma. Work beckoned, but how could they leave? Kellie would never forgive

40

herself, and he wasn't sure he'd be able to either.

Nathan glanced at his watch one more time. 7:56 a.m. He toyed with the idea of calling his office while he had the chance. So many things remained undone. The pressures were greater than ever. And yet he must stay here, at his wife's side. She needed him. And, in so many ways, Kellie's mother needed her. Norah Conway was one of the strongest women he had ever met, but she clearly longed to have her daughter nearby at a time like this.

Lord, You're going to have to work out the details. I've got too much on my plate to figure it all out.

Peace eluded him at the moment. With so much going on, he would truly have to hand this situation over to the Lord. Not that Nathan could fix it anyway. But it would surely feel better to relieve himself of the responsibility.

Over the next few minutes, as Kellie continued her phone conversation, Nathan came to a difficult decision. No matter what, he would do all he could to support Kellie and her family during this difficult time. No sacrifice was too great.

He came to another conclusion, as well.

He would hold her closer than ever. He would redeem every moment.

CHAPTER 4

Kellie stared at her reflection in the tiny restroom mirror and grimaced. The bags under her eyes grew larger daily. Each morning she attempted to swipe on a bit of eye shadow and mascara, but it seemed so pointless now. For nearly forty-eight hours, she had barely slept. Instead, she and Nathan shuffled in and out of the neurological ICU alongside her mother.

She occasionally gathered her wits about her long enough to think about what she might be missing at the office. Even then, she couldn't keep her thoughts straight. What did it matter anyway? Her father's life hung in the balance. How could she even justify thinking about fluctuations in the stock market or the potential loss of a client? What if she lost her father?

The news about his condition had fluctuated, as well — sometimes up, sometimes down. Her emotions seemed to follow suit, though she struggled hour by hour to call on God. *Where is my faith? I'm a spiritual wimp.* Still, she managed to garner up enough fortitude to face her mother with her chin up each and every time. She needed to be strong for her.

At least today things appeared more hopeful. With the bleeding under control, the swelling in her father's brain was receding. This was the first good news they'd had all along. And she clung to it with a fierceness that would not relent.

Soon — perhaps in the next few days — the doctors would allow him to rouse ever so gently from the medically induced coma they'd kept him in since his surgery. When the moment came, she would be right there at his side, even if it meant losing her job. Even if it meant going without sleep until they had some news.

Kellie exited the bathroom, gripping the doorknob with a paper towel in her hand. No point in taking chances. Not here, with so many germs floating around. She walked out into the hallway and stretched. Nathan approached her and wrapped her in his arms.

"I'm sure I smell just awful." She looked up into his understanding eyes.

Nathan shook his head and shrugged. "No

more so than the rest of us."

She yawned. "Mom says you and I should sneak over to her place and take a shower. Maybe even try to sleep a few hours. What do you think?"

"I, uh . . ." He pulled back and shifted his gaze.

"What?"

Nathan's words were quiet but rushed. "I hate to say this. I really do. But I've got to get back to the office. They're falling apart without me." He paused. "Well, not falling apart literally — but they act as if they are. My whole department is in turmoil."

Kellie didn't respond at first. She fought to push down the growing lump in her throat as she leaned her head against her husband's chest. She didn't want him to leave. She needed him, more than ever. "I wish you wouldn't —" She stopped midsentence. Why inflict guilt unnecessarily?

"I know. But it won't be so bad. I was thinking I could go back for a couple of days and get caught up, then come back to your mom's place. Sound okay?"

Not really. But I understand. "You have to do what you have to do." She pulled away from him and shrugged. "I'll be fine." She felt silly pouting but couldn't seem to help herself. After all, she was missing work, too.

Didn't he see that?

"If it would make you feel better, I could drive back and forth," he explained. "That way I could still spend time with you in the evenings."

"That doesn't make any sense," she argued. "You need your sleep if you're going to work. You can't work all day then come up here and stay awake all night. How would you drive back the next morning?"

"You need some rest, too." He reached to brush a stray hair out of her eyes. "I know you've got to be exhausted. At least I've slept a little in the waiting room. You haven't rested for days."

"I know." She sighed. "But every time I think about relaxing, I start to worry. What if I went home for a shower and Dad woke up? What if something happened to him and I was asleep?"

Nathan shook his head. "You can't control any of that. And besides, you put way too much on yourself. You always have."

She argued with herself before responding. When she did speak, the words came out sounding terse. She didn't mean for them to. She couldn't seem to control the emotion behind the explanation.

"You don't understand, Nathan." She crossed her arms at her chest. "I'm all they have. Ever since my sister moved to New York, I've been the logical choice. I have to be the one to pick up the slack."

"I know, but you can't be everything to everyone. You have to take care of yourself, or you won't be any good to your mom. And it's not as if she'd be alone." His face lit up with that slow, crooked grin she loved. "You've seen all her friends from church. At least three or four of them at a time are always here, tending to her every need."

"I know." Kellie sighed because he clearly didn't see her point. "It's just that . . ." It's just that her schedule at work had prevented her from spending enough time with her parents, and the guilt was eating at her like nothing she'd ever known.

"You don't have to be a superhero." He pulled her close once again and ran his fingers through her hair.

"I know." Tears welled up, and she let them travel in little rivers down her cheeks. "But I don't know how to rest. It goes against my nature. You know what a 'Martha' I am."

He smiled. "Yes, I know. But Jesus would have preferred that she sit at His feet like her sister, remember?"

I could tell you the same thing. You work just as hard. Maybe harder.

"I'll follow you and your mom out to her place," he said. "And then I'll head home to get some work done. Just a couple of days, honey. Then I'll come back."

She nodded. "It's fine." As the words were spoken, an unusual peace washed over her. It was fine. God was in control, and He would remain in control whether Nathan stayed or went. *Our love for each other is stronger than any separation. And God's love for both of us is even greater than that.*

Nathan glanced at his watch. "The next visitation time is in ten minutes. I won't leave until I've had a chance to see your dad once more. I want to pray with him before I go."

"Okay." She whispered the word and gave the situation over to the Lord.

She and Nathan went in search of her mother. They found her in the waiting room with three of the ladies from her church. All four women were huddled in a circle, praying and crying. For two days it had been like this. People from the small congregation had been a consistent part of the process for her mother. They wouldn't leave her side. They brought everything from fast food to casseroles, blankets to pillows, and devotion books to printed lists of God's promises. They prayed consistently, loved consistently, and gave consistently.

Kellie remembered this kind of love. As a child she had always known it. *Funny.* She hadn't appreciated it then. But now she missed it with an ache that couldn't be squelched.

Lord, will I ever experience true friendship again? I barely know anyone at my church. Who would take care of us if something like this happened? She pushed the thoughts from her mind. *Don't be selfish. Be glad they're here for Mom. That's the important thing.*

She and Nathan slipped across the hallway to the doors of the ICU. They used the hand sanitizer pump on the wall as they waited for the doors to swing open. When they did, Kellie was the first one inside. She had to get to her daddy, had to let him know she was still here, still praying. She had to see his face, to reassure herself he would be okay.

Nathan gripped her hand as they made their way across the crowded room to the bed where her father lay, still and silent. The bed was surrounded with monitors and IV poles. The light clicking sound continued on the monitor as his heart beat, steady and strong. She checked the numbers on the monitor to see if the pressure in his brain had subsided.

Funny how much she had learned in such a short time.

Sadly his numbers remained unchanged. She pressed back the lump in her throat and reached to take her father's hand. "Daddy, we're here. We love you." Salty tears slipped down her cheek and dribbled across her lip, but she swept them away. *No sadness here. Only hope.*

Nathan wrapped his arm around her waist and pulled her to him. She drew in a deep breath and continued. "You have a lot of friends here, Daddy. Half the church has come by to be with Mom and to let you know how much they love you. People are praying in the hallways, praying in the waiting room —"

"And praying right here." Nathan took a step closer to the bed and reached out his hand to touch her father's arm. In a voice quiet and genuine, he began to pray aloud. Kellie couldn't remember when she had ever heard him speak with such faith, such assurance, and even boldness.

And yet here he stood, taking a position of authority at the very moment when she needed him most. He finished the prayer, and she added her "amen" to his. She noticed another, quieter voice behind them and turned.

"Mom." She took her mother's hand and drew her closer to the bed. "I'm sorry. We thought you were still in the waiting room with your friends. I hope you don't mind that I rushed in ahead of everyone. I couldn't wait."

"Of course not." Her mother smiled. "I'm so glad you did."

Kellie noticed how tired her mother looked — and older than she could ever remember. She saw the pain in her mom's weary eyes and wanted to do something about it — but what could she do?

"You're doing what I've called you to do."

She started as she heard the words resound in her spirit. *Yes, Lord.*

The three of them stayed for a few minutes until a nurse with a brusque voice reminded them they were limited to two visitors at a time.

"I have to go anyway." Nathan planted a kiss on Kellie's head, then reached to grab her mother's hand. "I hope you don't mind, Mom, but I have to get to the office for a few days. I'll come back on the weekend."

"Of course I don't mind. You've been more than wonderful to come and stay as long as you have. It's far more than I would have expected, and I'm so grateful."

51

"I wouldn't have been anywhere else," Nathan said. He gave her a hug, then turned to Kellie.

Kellie's mom gave her a serious once-over. "You should take this girl with you. I'm sure she could use some rest."

"Mom, I'm not going home. I'll be fine." Kellie wasn't trying to be stubborn. She couldn't imagine leaving.

Nathan shook his head. "You're not fine — at least you won't be if you don't get some rest." He turned to face her mother. "I'm sending her to your place for a few hours to get some sleep. And a shower."

Kellie rolled her eyes. "He thinks I smell."

"I'm sure we all do." Her mother chuckled. "Speaking of which, if you're going to my place, I could use a change of clothes." She gave Kellie a list of items to fetch, and good-byes were said.

Kellie and Nathan left the hospital arm in arm. As she climbed into her mother's older-model sedan, she glanced in the rear-view mirror. Nathan gave her a smile and a wave from the driver's seat of her sports car.

With tears in her eyes, Kellie turned the key in the ignition and put her mother's car in gear. For once she would have traded it all — the job, the condo, the car, everything

52

— for a few more minutes with the man she loved.

Nathan shifted his wife's car into gear and headed out onto the highway toward Houston. He tried to still his thoughts, but they would not be silenced. Guilt ate at him like a cancer. How could he leave her there? Would she think his job took precedence over her? It wasn't true, but how could he prove it? Did he need to try?

Is my job too important? Have I focused too much on what's going on at the office and not enough on what's happening at home? He shook his head and concentrated on the road. A man had to work. And he had done a pretty good job of balancing his work life and home life.

Nathan prayed aloud as he clutched the steering wheel. "Lord, I know You've called me to provide for my family. Kellie is my family. I won't be able to provide for her if I lose my job." He drew in a deep breath. "Please give me wisdom. And please show me how to spend more time with her. I want to be with her."

I need to be with her.

He swallowed the lump in his throat and kept driving. His thoughts shifted to the office. With this current quarter drawing to a close, the workload was unbelievable. And for some reason tempers flared — even over the phone. The atmosphere of the whole place seemed to be changing right before his eyes. "It's the pressure of the season we're in. This is going to pass."

He hoped.

In the meantime, work waited. Balancing the phone in one hand and the steering wheel in the other, he punched in the number to his office.

CHAPTER 5

Kellie hung up the phone and turned to her mother with a sigh.

"Everything okay at work?" Her mom's forehead wrinkled in concern.

"I guess." Kellie took a seat at the breakfast table and nibbled at a piece of toast. Things weren't going as well as she'd hoped, but she certainly didn't want to concern her mother with unnecessary details. Her boss called every hour on the hour. Not to worry her, he insisted, but to keep her abreast of all she was missing.

Missing . . .

She fought to swallow the lump in her throat. She missed her husband with an ache that wouldn't subside. Though she had tried valiantly to sleep, she'd spent much of the last few nights tossing and turning. How could she sleep without Nathan by her side? Three years of marriage and they'd spent only four or five nights apart. And now this.

Her mother lifted a fried egg out of the skillet on the stove and slipped it onto her plate. "I'm sure I'll be fine, Kellie. You should go back home — at least for a few days."

"I can't do that, Mama. What if —" She stopped herself. In the four days since Nathan had returned home, she'd watched her father lie quiet and still in a hospital bed. She had prayed more prayers, cried more tears, and paced more hallways than ever before in her life.

And the prayers appeared to be working. His numbers had dropped substantially — enough for the doctors to pull him out of the medically induced coma. Anytime now, they predicted, her father should begin to awaken. What would happen after that was far more questionable. Regardless, she must be here — at her mother's side.

And yet . . .

Kellie's heart ached, and she brushed away the tears that clung to her lashes. She couldn't let her mother see her crying. The tears would have to be left to late-night hours, tumbling out onto crisp white pillowcases on the bed in her parents' guest room. They could never fall openly. If her mother knew how much Kellie's heart ached to be with Nathan, she would insist upon a rapid trip back to Houston.

Better to stay focused on the task at hand. "What time should we leave?" Kellie flashed a brave smile.

Her mother sat down across from her and took a bite of bacon. "Hmm." She glanced at the wall clock. "Probably about twenty minutes or so. Can you be ready that quick?"

"I'm the queen of quick." Kellie couldn't help but chuckle. "You have no idea how fast I can move, Mom."

"Oh, I can imagine. You've always been an overachiever, trust me. But you get that from your dad, not me. I'm a little simpler than that, as you know. Greenvine is the perfect place for a gal like me. We're pretty laid back around here. Just how I like it."

Kellie reflected on her words before responding. "I don't miss the fast-paced life as much as I thought I would, to be honest. It's weird — not having to set my alarm clock to be up before daylight. And I can't remember when I've had a real breakfast." She took another bite of toast and leaned back against the chair, happy for a few minutes of rest and relaxation.

"I've never known anything but this life." Her mother took a sip of her coffee, then continued, "Guess that's what happens when you've settled on a small-town environment. Life is slow. Simple. There's plenty of time to enjoy people — and things. Time to intercede for those who need it. And time to visit folks who need visiting."

Kellie shrugged. "Life is a lot slower here," she acknowledged. "I had almost forgotten."

"You didn't seem to mind when you were growing up," her mother said with a smile. "But I think your father and I always knew you'd end up in the big city."

"Really? What made you think that?"

"You seemed" — her mother gestured with her hands — "bigger than this place. You and your sister both. She was destined to sing in the opera, and you —"

"What?" Kellie couldn't help but wonder what she'd say next.

"You were so good with numbers. A real math whiz. And talk about saving money. Do you remember that piggy bank you had when you were little?"

"Yes." Kellie leaned her head down against the table. "Don't remind me." She couldn't help but smile as she thought about the bright pink ceramic pig with hand-painted eyelashes she'd received on her sixth birthday. She'd saved every penny that came her way, pressing each coin, each bill, through the narrow slot on his back.

"All of your birthday money, any cash you earned doing chores — you socked it all away in that little piggy bank."

Kellie shrugged. "Yes, but if memory serves me correctly, the payoff wasn't very good."

"That's right." Her mother's eyes narrowed to a slit. "You lost it."

"Not exactly *lost*. Misplaced would be the right word." Truth be told, she had hidden the ceramic pig away in a safe place once his belly had been stuffed full of money. She didn't want to run the risk of someone walking off with him. In the end she'd done the goofiest thing an eight-year-old kid could do — forgotten where she put it.

"We searched for that piggy bank for years, didn't we?"

"Yeah." Kellie sighed as she picked up the piece of toast again. "Lost forever."

"You learned a hard lesson from that, to be sure." Her mother smiled. "But a good one. Made you a lot less selfish with your money." She clamped her hand over her mouth, obviously embarrassed. "I'm sorry. Selfish might've been a strong word."

"No, that's about right." Kellie frowned as she contemplated her mother's words. She had been selfish as a child, perhaps more than she'd realized. And as an adult . . .

Am I still selfish? Is that why I work so hard — to put as much money into my "piggy bank" as I can?

She shrugged. "I'd like to think I've outgrown a lot of that, but I'm not sure. I do enjoy working, but it seems as if I spend a lot of time at the office."

"You're a hard worker, that's for sure." Her mother reached to squeeze her hand. "You always have been. That's nothing to be ashamed of. And I'm happy that you're happy." Her eyes misted over. "Both of my girls are doing what they love."

Am I? Kellie bit her lip. In her heart she wasn't sure. All the work earned a great lifestyle, but what good was a great lifestyle when you were too worn out to enjoy it?

"What, honey?"

"It's not that I don't love my work. I do. I really do."

"It's important to have an occupation you enjoy." Her mother gave her hand another gentle squeeze. "But I think I know what's bothering you."

"You do?"

Her mother nodded. "Remember to take time for yourself and Nathan. Don't let the work dictate who you are."

"I hadn't thought about it like that before." *I've always been Kellie the stockbroker. Not Kellie the woman or Kellie the wife or Kellie the child of God. Just Kellie . . . the stockbroker. The overachiever. The one who has to prove something to everyone.* The revelation nearly took her breath away.

They finished their breakfast in quiet contemplation, then left for Brenham. With her mother behind the wheel of the small sedan, Kellie took the opportunity to call Nathan.

He sounded thrilled to hear her voice. "Is that really you?"

Kellie felt the corners of her lips curl up. "Do you miss me?"

"Like crazy. I've been really . . ." He hesitated, then spoke in hushed tones, almost sounding embarrassed. "Lonely."

Kellie felt the familiar lump in her throat and fought to push it down so he wouldn't notice the pain behind her words. "Me, too."

His voice softened more but carried a hint of mischief. "I miss sleeping in the same bed with you."

"Me, too," she whispered.

"I miss you curling up next to me on my side of the bed — crowding me out."

Me, too.

"But most of all," he said a bit louder now, "I miss your snoring. I haven't slept a wink for days — it's been so quiet."

She groaned. "Hey, what's up with that?" She shook her head in disbelief. "I don't snore."

"Sure you don't." Nathan chuckled. "But the nights have been the hardest."

Kellie sighed. "I agree."

"We'll make up for it tonight. I'll be there by seven thirty at the latest."

"Why so late?"

"I have a lunch appointment and two afternoon meetings. I should be able to get out of here by five, but then I have to swing by our place and load up the car."

"Ah. Speaking of which, did you get that list of things I need from the condo?" Kellie thought back over the e-mail she'd sent the night before. Had she left anything out?

"I almost ran out of ink printing up the list. And I'll have to rent a moving truck to get it all to you."

She sniggered. "Very funny. It's only a few things."

His voice changed a little, and a seriousness took hold of the conversation. "How is your dad? Any changes?"

"Nothing" — she glanced at her mother and chose her next words carefully — "nothing significant."

"I don't know when I've ever prayed more

in my life."

"Same here," she confessed. In truth, she had devoted hours each night to prayer.

Nathan sighed. "I was hopeful he'd be awake by now."

"I know." She checked on her mother out of the corner of her eye. "Me, too."

"Well, I'm certainly bringing enough stuff for you to stay at least a week or two." He paused. "Did you talk to Mr. Weston about getting some work done from up there?"

"I did." Not that she wanted to talk — or think — about work.

"What did he say?"

"He told me to take a couple more days to see how my dad's doing. Then, if it looks like I'll have to stay longer, he'll give me the go-ahead. I think he's more worried about me than the business, to be honest. At least he sounded like it. And he knows Bernie can take care of my people while I'm gone. If you don't mind the fact that I'm not picking up any new clients, I'm certainly content to stay for now." She had barely missed her life at the brokerage. If only she and Nathan could be together, she would almost be at peace here awhile longer.

"Of course I don't mind. And I'm glad Weston wants you to take a little more personal time. You need it."

"I know."

"Things are a little more complicated here." Nathan's voice seemed to tighten as he talked about his job. "Tempers are rising, and problems are escalating. Nothing I'm in the center of — I'm thankful for that — but all the same, it's been pretty tense around the office ever since I got back. I sure don't think I could get away with being gone too long."

Kellie tried to focus on the good. "I understand. But you can stay all weekend. That's all that matters."

"Yes." He paused, then rushed through the next few words. "That's my other line. I'll call you when I get on the road, okay? I love you, baby."

"I love you more." She whispered the words, then snapped the phone shut. With tears she could no longer disguise, Kellie leaned her head back against the seat and turned her face to the window. She began the arduous task of counting the minutes until she would see her husband again.

Just as she began to lose herself in the emotion, Kellie's phone rang out. Her hands trembled the moment she recognized the number on the caller ID. With a fresh sense of fear gripping her heart, she glanced across the front seat at her mother, then spoke the necessary words. "Mom, it's the hospital."

Nathan drove toward Brenham in a frenzy. Kellie's rushed call from the hospital had been enough to cause him to cancel both afternoon meetings and come right away. He had quickly put together a bag of clothing items from her list but felt sure he'd left something out.

Not that it mattered. All that mattered now was getting to Brenham. He pulled off the highway at a quarter till four. Five minutes later, he drove into the crowded parking lot of the hospital. By four o'clock straight up, he was standing at the door of the ICU, preparing to go inside. Kellie stood alongside him, hand tightly gripped in his own.

"When did they call you?" he asked.

Her fingers twisted nervously inside his palm. "It was after I hung up from talking to you this morning."

"And what did they say again? Tell me every word."

"They —" She started to explain as the doors to the ICU opened and a nurse ushered them inside. Nathan followed along behind Kellie and her mother to his father-in-law's bedside. From outward appearances, nothing seemed to have changed.

And yet everything had changed.

"Daddy?" Kellie spoke softly at first, then a bit louder. "Daddy, you have visitors."

Nathan watched in stunned silence as his father-in-law's eyelids fluttered open then shut — open then shut again.

"Can you hear me, Kenton?" Norah implored. "If you can hear me, squeeze my hand twice."

They all looked on in shocked amazement as he slowly squeezed her hand two separate times. Tears rushed down Kellie's cheeks, and Nathan felt as if his heart would leap from his chest. *It's true. He's awake.*

For nearly twenty minutes, with tears in every eye, they celebrated the quiet victory. Nathan watched in awe. Though his father-in-law couldn't seem to formulate words, the older man's mind was clearly at work. Moisture brimmed his lashes as each person communicated their love and well wishes.

By the time they left the ICU, Nathan had little doubt his father-in-law would recover. The only question now was how long it would take. Regardless, he would do all he could to lend support, knowing that was exactly what any one of them would have done for him.

They drove back to his in-laws' house to

spend the night. Along the way, Nathan couldn't drop the nagging feeling that he'd left something at home — something important. It wasn't until they arrived at the house and Kellie asked about her laptop that he realized what it was.

CHAPTER 6

Kellie opened the front door to her condo and tentatively stepped inside. For some reason, she expected it to look different — more inviting maybe. Instead, it felt oddly cold. *I've been away too long.*

Ten days, to be exact. Ten long, exhausting days — days filled with prayers and fear, conversation and hope. Days filled with more time to think clearly than she could remember in a long time.

She dropped the stack of mail on the kitchen countertop and stepped back to look over her home. Sooner or later she would feel right about being here again. In the meantime, something felt off, odd.

"What's that smell?" She looked around, nose wrinkled. *Ah.* They must have exterminated while she'd been away.

No doubt many things had happened while she was in Greenvine. The first thing to tackle would be the monstrous stack of mail on the kitchen counter. She gave it a quick glance. *Bills. Ads. Junk, mostly.* One caught her eye, however. She ripped open an envelope and glanced at her bank statement inside. Her heart lifted as she took in the total. "Not bad, not bad."

"Everything okay?" Nathan appeared at the door, her luggage in hand.

She set the envelope back down. "Yep. Thought I'd lost you."

"After I dropped you off up front, I headed to the parking garage. But I had a whopper of a time finding a spot. If you can believe it, I had to park on the top floor."

"Again? Who took our spot?"

"The guy in 712. Want me to report him?"

Kellie sighed. "It won't do any good."

"You're right." He smiled. "I see you got the mail." Nathan gestured toward the countertop. "Should we sort through it tonight?"

"I already did. Nothing that can't wait till morning. I'm too tired to mess with bills tonight, to be honest."

"I hear ya." Nathan carried her luggage into the bedroom and lifted the larger suitcase onto the bed.

Kellie followed behind him and opened it right away. "I'm sure my clothes are a wrinkled mess." She groaned as she pulled out the soft green designer blouse on top. *Ninety dollars — and look at it.*

"I need to make a run to the dry cleaners anyway," Nathan said. "I'll be glad to drop off your things, too."

"You're awesome." She gave him a kiss on the cheek, and he drew her close.

"You know, you could do this in the morning." He gestured toward the suitcase. "I can think of a lot of things I'd rather do than unpack laundry."

Kellie tried to avoid his gray blue eyes. "I know. Me, too."

He whispered in her ear, "I've missed you, Kellie. It just hasn't been the same without you."

"I know." She planted tender kisses on his cheek. "It's been awful."

"I don't know how people manage," he said. "I could never be one of those husbands who had to travel all the time. It would drive me crazy to be away from you."

She sighed. "It couldn't be helped. I needed to be there. And I'm going to have to go back — at least on the weekends. As long as Daddy's in rehab, my mom's going to need me. It could be weeks. Even longer maybe." Her heart twisted with the words. Even now she longed to get in the car and head back to where they'd come from.

"I know. And I'll be there with you as much as I can," he said. "But your mom had a long talk with me. She's concerned that you're missing so much work. I think she feels a little guilty about it."

"I hope I didn't make her feel that way." Kellie pulled back a step, deep in thought. "It probably didn't help that Mr. Weston called so much. He was an ever-present reminder, I'm afraid."

She sat on the edge of the bed and contemplated this revelation. *But she's right. I do need to go back to work.* To stay away much longer could potentially put at risk all the well-laid financial plans she and Nathan had settled on. If they didn't meet their financial goals, they would have to put off their dreams of buying a house — and having a child — even longer.

Nathan continued, clearly oblivious to her ponderings. "Your mom wants the best for everyone," he said. "For your dad, for you . . ." He paused and looked into her eyes with some concern. "She's so used to taking care of everyone. I'm sure it must feel odd that everyone is now sweeping in to take care of her."

"She needs it. I'm so glad Katie was able to fly down for a few days. Otherwise I don't think I could have left." Kellie reached to pull a gray skirt from the suitcase. *Great. This one has to go to the dry cleaners, too.*

"True. And you've been there for her every step of the way. But doesn't it feel great to be home again?"

She looked around the familiar bedroom and nodded. There was a certain comfort to this place — a familiarity. In spite of the smell. In spite of the pull to be elsewhere. This was still home.

"Now" — he zipped the suitcase closed and lifted it down onto the floor — "what do you say we forget about dirty clothes and parking spaces for a while and focus on us?"

"I think" — she gave him a teasing look — "that sounds perfect."

In the days that followed Kellie's return to Houston, Nathan watched over her closer than ever before. He couldn't help it. Something in her demeanor had changed. Sure, she had settled in at the condominium. She had even returned to work with a vengeance. But something was — off. He could feel it.

Daily she called her mother for an update. The news remained unchanged for the most part. Though her father had been transferred to a rehab facility, his recovery would be slow, tedious. Kenton could put together a few words but would have to relearn how to function in most every area of life.

"I can't even imagine." Nathan voiced his thoughts aloud as he eased his car through traffic on Houston's busy 610 loop. To lose your ability to function, to work . . .

How could a person reenter the job force after something like that? Would Kenton ever return to his job? Would his God-given skills regenerate, or was he destined to live a half-life? Nathan shrugged that idea aside. Of course his father-in-law would make a full recovery. They wouldn't give up on praying for that very thing.

As he reached the Post Oak exit, Nathan wound his way through the cars and counted the minutes until he arrived at the restaurant where Kellie probably already waited. He had planned tonight's outing with much anticipation. After so much time apart, he now chose to take advantage of each moment.

He pulled up to the valet parking at Le Jardin, one of Houston's classiest restaurants, known for its tempting French cuisine. After handing over the keys, he sprinted toward the door. He reached in his pocket to feel for the familiar jewelry box. In a few moments he would draw it from its hiding place and set it on the table in front of the most wonderful woman in the world.

The host led Nathan to a small table in the back of the restaurant where Kellie waited. She sat with her laptop open, typing with a vengeance.

"Hey, baby." He kissed her on the forehead.

She started, then looked up into his eyes with a smile. "Hey. Just catching up on some work. Can you believe they have wireless Internet access in a place like this?"

"I believe it." He shook his head. "It's scary, but I believe it." He smiled at his beautiful bride. "So, how are things at the office? Getting settled back in?"

She groaned. "This probably wouldn't be the day to ask."

"Ah. Well, things are finally slowing down for me. I was able to sneak away to the health club for an hour this afternoon."

"Good for you. I'm going to try to do that tomorrow. I haven't worked out in weeks. And with all the food my mom's friends brought in, I've probably added at least three inches to these hips of mine." She flashed him an impish grin. "I don't think I've ever seen so much fried chicken in my life. Or cakes. Have you ever seen that many cakes in one place?"

Nathan's heart twisted. *Lord, how long has*

it been since I've seen her smile like that? "The food was great, but you haven't changed a bit. You look terrific."

"Thanks, baby." Kellie snapped her laptop shut and picked up a menu. "But all this talk about my ever-widening hips has reminded me — I'm starving! What sounds good to you?"

"I don't know. Let's have a look." They settled on lobster bisque and steak with béarnaise sauce.

Once their waiter — a stocky fellow with a contrived French accent — disappeared, they sat in silence a moment. *The clinking of silverware and soothing instrumental music provides the perfect backdrop,* Nathan reasoned. He and Kellie would enjoy an intimate meal together and fill the empty spaces with conversation that excluded work-related things.

"I haven't been here in ages." Kellie looked around the room in quiet contemplation.

"Me either. It seems like we're always eating on the run." Nathan garnered up the courage to continue. "In fact, that's one of the reasons I wanted tonight to be so special. I wanted to let you know I think we should have a regular date night."

She smiled. "That's a nice idea. I'll take a

75

look at my calendar and pencil you in." She was teasing, but something about her words bothered him.

"No." He felt his lips curl down. "We have to stop fitting each other in. We have to make sure we put our relationship above our jobs."

"Wow." She took hold of his hand and squeezed it. "That sounds like something I had planned to say to you tonight. I don't know how much longer I can go on with things the way they've been. I mean, what's the point of having great jobs, a great place to live, and all that if we hardly have time to see each other?"

"Amen." He flashed a broad, heartfelt smile. "Sounds like we've prepared the same speech." He paused and gazed into her eyes. "So what do you think we should do about that?"

She shrugged. "I like the date-night idea. It might be a little harder, now that we're driving back and forth to Greenvine every weekend. But I have Tuesday evenings free, for sure. What about you?"

"Tuesdays are good for me. At least for now." He pulled out his handheld PC to double-check. "Yep. That'll work."

"And we can take advantage of our drive time to my mom's place," she suggested.

"What do you mean?" Nathan's curiosity got the better of him.

"I mean" — she grinned mischievously — "we could spend that time talking. Really talking — about our hopes, our dreams, our innermost thoughts."

"Our innermost thoughts?" Nathan smiled. Kellie had such a definitive way with words.

"You know." Her gaze shifted to the table. "We need to talk about things like . . . children. When we're going to have them."

"Aha. *Those* innermost thoughts." Nathan nodded. "I agree." He reached into his pocket and grasped the tiny box. "But in the meantime, I have a few innermost thoughts of my own I'd like to share with you."

Her face flushed. "Right here?"

"I can't think of a better place." He stared into her eyes and shared his heart. "I love you, Kellie. I want you to know that. You're more important to me than anything else."

Her eyes filled with tears. "I love you, too, babe."

"I have something for you." He pulled the box up to the table and set it in front of her.

Kellie's eyes grew large. "What's this?"

"Open it and see." He could hardly wait

to see the look on her face.

Kellie tentatively lifted the lid to the box and gasped as she gazed at the diamond bracelet inside. It matched the necklace he'd given her on their wedding day. "Nathan!"

He stood and approached her side of the table. Reaching into the box, he pulled out the delicate bracelet and fastened it around her wrist. "You deserved something special. You've been through so much lately."

She looked a bit dazed. "But this is too much. . . ."

"Nothing is too much for you." He gripped her hand and spoke passionately. "I mean that, honey. You're the most valuable thing in the world to me. And there's nothing I could ever give you — nothing I could do — to show you how much you mean to me. This bracelet is a small attempt on my part to share something huge that's on my heart."

Tears ran in tiny rivers down her cheeks. "I love you," she whispered.

"I love you more." He winked in her direction. They turned their attentions to the meal and to one another. Nathan relaxed as they chatted back and forth. For the first time in weeks, he felt some sense of direction.

CHAPTER 7

Kellie stepped out of her father's private room at the rehab facility and leaned against the wall. She didn't like this place — the smells, the people in varying stages of brain damage, the nurses scurrying to and fro, caring for patients who often cried out in pain or shouted foul insults. They couldn't be blamed, of course, but it was too much to take in.

With her eyes brimming over, she stared at the door leading to her father's room. On the other side of that door, a man she barely recognized lay in a bed, fighting to relearn everything.

"Lord, I don't understand." How could he ever become the strong, intelligent man she had always known? And why was everything moving so slowly? She fought with her feelings, one moment up, the next down. Would this roller-coaster ride ever come to a satisfactory end, or were they destined to spend the rest of their lives loving a man who barely remembered his own name, let alone how to function in the world?

"Kellie?"

She looked up as her mother stepped out into the hall, and guilt overwhelmed her at once. She couldn't let anyone know her fears, her doubts. She must remain positive, upbeat — at all costs. Kellie brushed away the tears, ashamed to let her mother find her in a moment of weakness, and then offered up a smile. "What's up, Mom?"

"I'm concerned about you. Are you okay?"

Mom, you're always comforting me. It's supposed to be the other way around. I'm supposed to be helping you through this. "Everything is moving so slowly." Kellie sighed. "I wish we had some kind of button we could push to speed him through this."

"I know." Her mother smiled. "You're the queen of quick. I remember."

Kellie groaned. "I can't believe I said that."

"I guess some things can't be rushed." Her mother shrugged. "But while your dad's relearning, I suppose we'll have to learn a few things, too."

"I guess." Kellie paused. "It's just so hard to . . . to . . ." She choked back tears. "To

80

see him like this."

"I know." Her mother drew her into a tight embrace and whispered, "It's hard on all of us — but it has to be harder on him than anyone. I can't even imagine."

"I can't either. He's always been so strong. And his mind . . ." She pulled back and gazed into her mother's weary face. "He has the brightest mind of anyone I've ever known."

"That's what I'm counting on." Mom smiled. "I know he's still in there, honey. And he's fighting with all of his strength. I can see it in his eyes."

"I can, too." Kellie brushed away loose tears. "And I'm so proud of him. It's just so hard to watch. I don't know if I have it in me to make it through the emotional ups and downs. Sometimes I wonder . . . if things will ever be the same again." She paused as she examined her mother's face for a response. "Are you ashamed to hear me say that?"

"Ashamed?" Her mother's eyes watered. "Oh, honey, of course not. If anyone understands what you're thinking and feeling, I do. Trust me." Her mother took a seat. "I'm up here every day, watching. And praying. But that doesn't mean I don't get discouraged."

Up here every day. Kellie cringed. How she wished she could be here every day. How she longed to drop everything and race to her father's side as he walked through this valley. How guilty she felt for going about her daily work as if nothing had changed — when everything had changed.

"I'm relieved to hear you say that," Kellie confessed. "You're so full of faith. It helps to know you have your down moments, too."

"I don't think we'd be human if we didn't. It's not my faith I question. I have faith. I think we grow weary sometimes. But those are the times the Lord has to carry us — when we admit our weakness. We're completely dependent on Him."

"I know you're right. I hadn't thought it through like that." Kellie's spirits lifted at her mother's words. "And I know Daddy's getting better every day. He's taking baby steps, but every one is a step in the right direction."

"Yes," her mother agreed. "And he knows we're here, even when he can't voice his feelings. It means the world to him. I can see it in his eyes."

Kellie sat next to her mother, quiet for some time. "I wish I could be here more," she said finally. "It doesn't seem like enough to come on weekends." *It isn't enough.*

"Don't be so hard on yourself." Her mother patted her hand. "You have a husband and a job. Daddy understands that, even if he can't say it. We all do."

For some reason Kellie couldn't let the idea rest. In her heart she yearned to do more. In her heart she saw herself here — every day — alongside her mother. She wanted to play an important role in her father's healing. He needed her. "I could take some time off from work," she said, suddenly determined.

"But you've already done that." Kellie's mother gave her a quizzical look. "You've lost over a week's work already."

"No. I mean, I could take an extended leave of absence." Kellie paused, deep in thought. "Or better yet" — she felt her excitement rising — "I could work from here. I could focus on day-trading. As long as I have Internet access, I could make it work. I know I could."

"Day-trading?"

"Yes. I could work a few hours in the morning and then come up here for the rest of the day. I know I could handle the workload. My income might drop a little, but what difference would that make, in the grand scheme of things? And it's not as if I can't make up for it later. I can. I know I can."

"But what about Nathan?" Her mother's eyes registered concern. "Think about what you're saying, Kellie. You might be able to make it work for you, but it would be terrible for the two of you to be apart. I watched you try. It's not fair to him — or to you."

Kellie felt as if the wind had suddenly been knocked out of her sails. "I know." She sighed deeply. "If only we could find some way to —"

"To have your cake and eat it, too?"

Kellie looked up as she heard Nathan's quiet interjection. "Nathan. H–how long have you been standing there?"

"Awhile." He sat next to her and leaned his head back against the wall.

"I'm sorry," she whispered as she leaned her head against his shoulder. "I know I'm not making much sense."

"I understand, baby." He kissed her on the forehead. "This is hard."

She sighed. "Have you ever wished you could be in two places at once?"

Nathan pursed his lips. "Only when you were here and I was at home alone. I wished it every day."

She dropped the subject. "I'm sorry. I

know it's impossible. Just wishful thinking on my part."

"No harm in that." He slipped an arm around her shoulders. "I wish I had the answer for you. I really do. But we'll keep praying. God will give us direction. I know He will. And in the meantime, we'll keep coming every weekend. We'll be here as often as we can."

Kellie nodded. *Lord, I wish I had his faith.* She looked up as Dr. Koenig, her father's neurologist, joined them in the hallway. He spoke in hushed tones, as if somehow that would shield her father from whatever he had to say. In truth, Kellie had to admit, her father probably wouldn't make much sense of their conversation, regardless of the volume.

Dr. Koenig gave them a sympathetic smile. "I know you're anxious to see him progress."

Everyone nodded in agreement. Kellie gripped Nathan's hand in her own.

"The truth is, he is progressing, even if it's not apparent to the naked eye," the doctor continued. "We can't discount how far he's already come. The fact that he's awake and able to move is very hopeful. And his ability to speak, albeit only a few words, is also a good sign."

Kellie fought to push thoughts of frustration from her mind. The few slurred words coming from her father sounded little like the man she knew and loved. "How long?" She voiced the question everyone surely wondered. "How long will he be in here? How long before he's back to . . . to normal?"

Dr. Koenig drew in a breath and looked her squarely in the eye. "I wish I could answer that. I do." He paused and shook his head. "Some of my neurological patients enter the rehab in dire straits, then end up staying only a few weeks. They leave as if nothing had ever happened. And then . . ."

Kellie glanced up as he gestured to the recreation hall, where patients with varying degrees of neurological problems visited together. Some watched television. Others struggled to stand, to walk. Some swore at nurses and shouted insults to those walking by. Still others sat in silence in their wheelchairs, staring out of windows.

"Some of my patients have been here quite some time," the doctor explained. "There's truly no way to predict. It's too soon to tell how quickly Kenton will progress. But I'm very hopeful. And he needs you to be, also."

"We are." Kellie's mother reached out and

placed her hand on the doctor's arm. "We're not going to give up, and neither is he. I know that man of mine. He's a fighter. He wants to get through this."

Kellie felt the familiar lump rise into her throat. She tried to push it down as she spoke. "We're going to be here for him."

"That's the key thing." Dr. Koenig smiled warmly. "He will respond to the familiar. The more time you can spend with him, the better. I can't express how important that is. Having your support will be better than any medication I can give him."

Kellie noticed Nathan's palm grew sweaty in her own.

As the doctor turned to leave, she turned, as well. Kellie looked her husband in the eye and prepared herself to ask him for the impossible.

Nathan listened intently as he drove to his mother-in-law's house. Kellie's heartfelt words left little to the imagination. They brought to light feelings she had not fully voiced in the days prior, feelings he now struggled to reconcile with his own. With tears flowing, she poured out her heart, expressing her desire to stay in Greenvine so she could be closer to her father.

With a lump in his throat, Nathan fought

to respond. But what could he say? How could he reciprocate her feelings when he wasn't even sure he understood them? In truth, he couldn't make much sense out of Kellie's emotional request. Could she be serious? How could they settle in a town like Greenvine, even for a short period of time? And, if so, how could he go along with such a thing? How would they continue to work? What would happen to their condominium, their jobs, and their lifestyle?

He drove in silence, conscious of her breathing as the tears continued to fall. *Lord, help me. I don't want to blow this. Give me Your words to say.*

"I didn't know I would feel this strongly," Kellie explained with great passion. "I've never been through anything like this before. I don't have anything to compare it to."

"We're both on a learning curve," he acknowledged.

"I guess this whole experience has made me reconsider some things." She looked over at him with those sad eyes, and Nathan forced himself to stay focused on the road. He bit his lip and continued to drive.

"What kinds of things?"

"Things like fancy cars, expensive condominiums, and high-paying jobs," she said. "These days I spend more time thinking about the things that are really important — family, relationships, and quality time with the people I love — that sort of thing."

"I hear you." Nathan chose his words carefully. "And I agree that those things are more important. I don't see an answer to this problem, though, at least not one that would satisfy both of us. I know you want to be with your dad —"

"And with you," she said adamantly. "That's why the only way it would work is if we were in agreement. Together both physically and psychologically. But that means we'd both have to be willing to make some changes."

"I don't do change well," he said. "And, to be honest, I can't even imagine staying here. Your mom already has her hands full, and I don't think I'd want to give up my privacy by staying in her house. It just wouldn't feel like —"

"Like home?" she asked.

"Right. Home."

"I think I have a solution." Kellie smiled, and Nathan realized she had already come up with a plan, had already worked this out in her head. Without him.

"What's that?" He turned onto her mother's street and listened carefully as she explained.

Her eyes sparkled with excitement as she spoke. "What would you think about renting a house?"

"What?" He hit the brakes and pulled the car off to the side of the road so he could make sure he'd heard correctly. "Renting a house here? In Greenvine?"

Her energy level rose with each word. "Yes. I've given this a lot of thought, baby. There's a house for rent two blocks from here. At least I hope it's still available. I saw the sign out front last time we were here. It's so inexpensive that you're going to laugh when you hear how much they're asking."

"I doubt it." He pursed his lips.

"I know what you're thinking." She grabbed his hand and gazed at him with a look of desperation in her eyes. "You're thinking we won't be able to balance everything out. But I think we can do this, Nathan. I — I know we can." She raced ahead, nearly breathless. "I can work over the Internet. I can spend time with my mom and still have plenty of time with you in the evenings and on weekends. And it's not really that far for you to drive, is it?"

"Kellie, I don't know."

Her eyes widened more with each impassioned word. "I mean, an hour and a half each way . . . people do it every day. We could keep our condominium. Or rent it out. Whatever you think. I mean, we're only talking about a few months after all — not a lifetime."

He shook his head in disbelief. "I'm floored. I don't know what to say. It sounds as if you've got everything worked out, right down to the house. But you've completely left me out of the equation." He fought to keep his temper in check. How could she see this as an answer?

"I–I'm sorry." She lowered her head, and droplets of tears fell onto her blouse as she spoke in hushed tones. "You're right. I just don't know what else to do."

They sat in silence for some time before Nathan put the car in gear again. Try as he might, he couldn't think of anything to say. With a heavy heart, he turned the car in the direction of his mother-in-law's home.

CHAPTER 8

Kellie crossed the parking lot of the small community church with her husband's hand tightly clutched in her own. She smiled as she spied the new education building off to the left. Children raced across the sidewalk, scurrying from place to place. Not so many years ago, she had been one of them. "This place has grown," she said.

"It has?" Nathan looked around, clearly surprised.

Kellie had to laugh. "I know it doesn't look like much, but it's about twice the size it was when I was a kid. And my mom tells me they've renovated the sanctuary. I can hardly wait to see it." In truth, she could hardly wait to see the people inside the sanctuary. How many would remember her? How many would she still connect with?

They entered the building, and Kellie braced herself for the inevitable. Sure enough, as they crossed into the foyer, a host of people greeted them.

"Why, if it isn't little Kellie Conway!" An elderly woman grabbed her hand and squealed in glee.

"It's Kellie Fisher now, Mrs. Dennison." She smiled broadly as Nathan extended his hand. Her heart swelled with pride as she introduced him. "This is my husband, Nathan."

"Nathan." The older woman released her hold on Kellie and grasped Nathan's hand. She looked him in the eye. "Yes, I heard all about your wedding. Heard you did it up right. Folks 'round these parts aren't accustomed to such fancy to-dos, but we can't fault you for pulling out all the stops." Here she paused and gazed tenderly at Kellie. "She's worth it, after all. You have an amazing girl here. She was quite a little pistol as a child. I should know. I was her Sunday school teacher."

Kellie felt her cheeks flush. "Mrs. Dennison taught my Sunday school class for several years," she explained. "She took us all the way through the Old and New Testaments. We studied over a hundred Bible characters."

"Probably more," the older woman said. "And I could have taught much longer, but I had to retire after my hip surgery." She finally let go of Nathan's hand and smiled admiringly at the couple. "But I'll never forget this girl. She was our class treasurer her freshman year in high school. Took great care of the offerings."

Nathan smiled. "That doesn't surprise me."

"She was always a whiz with numbers," Mrs. Dennison continued. "Never quite figured out how she kept up with it all, but she devised some sort of system for keeping track of funds even before they came in."

Nathan chuckled. "That's my girl."

"I'm still working with numbers," Kellie explained. "I'm a stockbroker at a firm in the Houston area."

"I believe your mother told me that. We're so proud of you, honey." Mrs. Dennison beamed with joy. "Now me, I can barely balance my checkbook." She chuckled, but eventually a serious look returned to her face. "But speaking of your mother, is she here?"

"I believe she'll be here any moment now," Kellie explained. "She stopped off to see Dad on her way."

"I saw him myself this morning." Mrs. Dennison smiled. "I try to go by on Sunday mornings before church to pray with him. And, of course, Wednesday is my day to work crossword puzzles with him. He's always loved those crossword puzzles."

Wow. "I remember," Kellie said. "Thanks for spending so much time with him. I know it has to bless my mother to have all her friends close by."

"Well, that's what friends do, honey." Mrs. Dennison chuckled. "I wouldn't be able to look myself in the mirror each day if I didn't follow the leading of the Lord in times like these."

A man with white hair and a rounded belly interrupted their conversation. "How's your father, Kellie?"

She looked up into the eyes of Hal O'Keefe, her father's best friend.

"A little better, I think." Kellie grinned at the older man's familiar crooked smile. "We went to see him yesterday. Stayed a few hours. He's able to eat now, with help, of course. We're headed back over there today after the service."

"Well, I'll see you up there this afternoon then," he explained. "I always take communion to the shut-ins on Sundays."

"That's wonderful." *These people are amazing.*

"Hal and his wife have done more than their share. Everyone has." Kellie's mother interrupted their conversation with her thoughts on the matter, and Kellie smiled in her direction.

"Hi, Mom. How's Dad doing this morning?"

"Oh, about the same." Her mother shrugged. "But he wanted to make sure I passed along a message to his friends at the church. He's so grateful to you all." She spoke to the whole room now, and they responded with comforting smiles and nods in her direction. "You've brought so much food — I could never eat it all. You've gone above and beyond the call."

"Well, we love you and Kenton," Hal said. "When you love folks, you can never do too much for them."

Kellie marveled at their easy exchange, so intimate, and yet it sounded so foreign to her. The conversation swung in several different directions at once as people came in droves to inquire after her father's health and hug her. Kellie listened in stunned silence as her mother took the time to connect with each person personally. *Lord, she really knows how to love people.*

From inside the sanctuary the opening song began to play. Kellie turned to Nathan, who looked a little uncomfortable. "We'd better go get a seat."

He nodded, and they made their way inside.

The pianist began to play the first song, a triumphant melody Kellie recognized right away. The worship leader stood and encouraged the congregation to join him. All across the room, people stood, many reaching to hug a neighbor or family member as the first words were sung.

As the song continued, Kellie looked around the room. Many of the people had aged, no doubt, but many remained seemingly unchanged. She caught the eye of Julia, her best friend from high school, and gave a little wave. The pretty redhead held a sleeping child in her arms — a little girl with cherub cheeks and hair every bit as red as her mother's. Julia's husband, Frankie, sat to her right. For some reason Kellie's heart lurched as she watched the three of them together. She couldn't explain the feeling and tried to cast it off, choosing instead to concentrate on choir members, who sang jubilantly.

A feeling of comfort enveloped her, and she settled into the familiar routine. The service flew by. Kellie couldn't remember when she'd enjoyed church so much or when a message had impacted her more. She glanced at her watch as the final song was sung. *Noon.* Enough time to grab a bite to eat with her mom and then visit with her father for a couple of hours. She and Nathan would have to be back on the road by four in order to make it home in time to prepare for work tomorrow.

"Are you okay?" Nathan got her attention as the pew emptied out.

"Oh yes." She nodded. "Just thinking."

"About?"

"Oh, about all we have to do today."

"That's what I was thinking about, too." They stood and made their way through the crowd down the center aisle of the church. "I'd like to take care of something before we leave."

"Oh?" She wondered what he meant.

At that very moment, Julia approached with the baby in her arms. "Kellie. It's so great to see you again."

"You, too." She embraced her old friend. "And who's this little angel?"

Julia beamed with pride. "This is Madison. She's a year and a half now."

"Well, she's a beauty." Kellie ran her fingers through the child's soft curls. "And my mother tells me you have more news."

"Yes." Julia flashed an embarrassed smile and brushed her hand across her belly. "I found out eight weeks ago. The babies will be a little more than two years apart." She shook her head and giggled. "But I'm not complaining. I love being a mom. I think I was born for this."

Kellie felt the usual tug on her heart. "Well, if the next one is half as pretty as Madison, she'll be a doll."

"Thank you. But we're hoping for a boy."

Nathan squeezed Kellie's hand, and she took the hint. "I hate to leave so soon, but we're headed up to the rehab to see my dad."

"Give him my love, will you?" Julia said. "I'll be back up there on Tuesday. Your mom told me how much he loves reading the paper, so I try to spend a little time reading to him. And he loves seeing Madison. I'm pretty sure he remembers her; his face lights up every time I bring her in the room."

"Wow. That's great."

Julia shrugged. "It's the least I can do. Your parents have always been so wonderful to me." She paused as she gazed intently at Kellie. "Will I see you there?"

"No. I, uh . . ." Kellie's heart twisted once again. "I'll be back in Houston. I have to work."

"Oh, I'm sorry to hear that. But it was great to see you." Julia gave her a warm hug and turned to visit with others nearby.

Nathan and Kellie forced their way through the crowd in the foyer and then managed to make it out into the parking lot together.

"I never would have believed they could fit that many people into such a small space." Nathan gave the building an admiring glance. "I'm impressed."

"This place has been bursting at the seams for as long as I can remember." Kellie pulled her keys from her purse. "But even with the renovations, they're still pretty full. I wouldn't be surprised if they have to go to two services soon."

"Sounds logical."

They continued to chat as they crossed the parking lot. As they approached the car, Kellie extended her hand with the keys. "Would you like to drive? My mom wants us to meet her at the Country Buffet out on the highway."

"I don't mind." He took the keys. "But I was hoping to change your plans a little."

"What do you mean?" Surely he didn't want to leave for Houston right away.

"I mean," he said as he unlocked the car, "that I've given a lot of thought to what we were talking about yesterday."

"You — you have?" She bit her lip and waited for his next words.

Nathan opened her door and nodded. "I have." He paused, and his brow wrinkled a bit with his next words. "I don't have a permanent solution, but I'm willing to consider the idea of driving back and forth — at least for a while."

Kellie caught her breath. "You are?" She could hardly contain her excitement but didn't want to alarm him by responding with too much zeal. "Oh, Nathan. I know we can make it work. I know we can."

"One thing," he said firmly. "I don't want to rent out the condo. I'm sure we won't need to stay here that long. But I've been thinking about that house you told me about. I thought maybe we could swing by after lunch and take a look. Maybe, just maybe . . ."

Maybe. Kellie's heart sang. Maybe she *could* have her cake and eat it, too.

After lunch, Nathan pulled the car into the driveway of the rickety white house with the FOR RENT sign out front. It didn't look like much, but looks could be deceiving. He hoped.

With Kellie's fingers laced through his, they crossed the overgrown front yard and knocked on the door. Nathan tried to push aside the heaviness in his heart as they waited for someone to answer. He had wrestled with the Lord all night over this decision, but the Lord had eventually won out. Kellie was right. She needed to be here with her mother. And he needed to do whatever it took to make that possible. In spite of the daily drive. In spite of the concerns over the cost.

"Well, hey there." A large man, nearly as scruffy looking as the yard, answered the door with a suspicious grin. "What've we got here?" He rubbed at his whiskery jowl and took them in with a lingering gaze.

The whole thing made Nathan more than a little uncomfortable. "We've come to take a look at the house." He tried to sound self-assured as he spoke.

"Have you now?" The man's face lit up like an evergreen on Christmas morning, and suddenly there wasn't a frightening thing about him. "Well then, come on in. The name's Chuck Henderson, by the way." He extended his broad hand, and Nathan shook it warmly.

They entered the house, and Nathan knew right away why Chuck had opted to charge so little rent. The place was a disaster. The paneled walls appeared to be coming loose in places. The sofa, an old plaid number from the seventies, was threadbare. A large dog of the Heinz 57 variety lay stretched out across a broken recliner in a sound sleep.

"That's Killer." Chuck gestured toward the mutt. "He's my watchdog."

The monstrous creature rolled over and yawned, then dozed off again.

"Uh-huh." Nathan would have said more, if every word he'd ever known hadn't escaped him.

"He takes good care of this place."

"Right." It looked as if someone needed to take care of the place.

"What do you think?" Chuck spoke with his hands as he showed off the room. "It's really something, ain't it?"

Nathan nodded politely. "At the very least."

Kellie looked around, clearly stunned. "It's not exactly what I was expecting."

"Lots of folks say that." Chuck smiled. "It's big, ain't it?"

In comparison to a cracker box? Nathan tried to be open-minded, but logic prevented it.

"It don't look like much from the outside, but these rooms are bigger'n people expect," Chuck explained. "And look at that carpet."

I'm looking. Nathan stared in shocked silence at the dingy gold rug.

"You don't find shag carpet like that these days. Folks is laying down those noisy ceramic tiles or fake hardwoods." He took off his shoe and raked his toes through the carpet. "Nothing fake about this. And there ain't nothing like the feel of real shag between your toes." He flashed a contented smile and slipped his shoe back on.

Nathan couldn't seem to think of a response. Instead he and Kellie followed the fellow into the next room — the kitchen. The countertops, crafted of butcher block, were clearly worn down by the years. The appliances probably all dated back to the late sixties or early seventies. The cabinet doors hung from broken hinges, and the sink was filled with dirty dishes. In short, it was nearly the worst kitchen he'd ever laid eyes on. Or smelled, for that matter.

Nathan tried to read Kellie's mind. *She's used to granite countertops, top-of-the-line appliances, hardwood floors. Surely she'll see this would never work.*

His beautiful wife looked the place over in complete silence. He couldn't seem to read her thoughts.

"We got three bedrooms here." Chuck led the way down a narrow hallway to a door on the left. "The first one is kinda small. My daughter tells me it'd make a great office. I've been using it for storage." He pushed the door open, and Nathan gasped.

Storage? The room was filled, top to bottom, with junk. Nathan could hardly believe his eyes.

"Wow." Kellie mouthed the word, her eyes widening.

"If you liked that, you'll love the next room." Chuck led them down the hall to a second small bedroom, equally as messy. "This one's bigger. You two could put a baby in here."

Never in a million years would I put a child in that room.

"Well, we don't have any children," Kellie explained. Her cheeks flushed bright red.

"I can't wait for you to see this." Chuck grinned as he pushed open the door to the master bedroom, and for the first time, Nathan noticed a tooth missing on the upper right. "The master suite — fit for a king and queen."

Together they entered a room that was surprisingly big — and not terribly hard on the cyes. It needed a fresh coat of paint, but this was the only place in the entire house Nathan could see himself in. For a few moments, anyway.

"What about the bathrooms?" Kellie asked the question quietly, and Nathan tried to imagine what she must be thinking about all of this.

Chuck led them through the bedroom to the master bath. It was dated and in much need of cleaning. The discolored tiles appeared to be coming loose from around the tub, and the grout had fallen in clumps.

"Wow." Nathan made use of his one-word vocabulary again.

"Yep. She's a beauty." Chuck turned on the light and gestured to the shower. "Now that showerhead is new. I bought it at the hardware store and installed it myself. It's a fancy one."

Nathan nodded silently.

"So what do you think?" Chuck looked him squarely in the eye. " 'Cause I've got another couple interested."

Sure you do. "Well —" Nathan looked at Kellie to gauge her thoughts.

She stared at the room with interest. "Would you let us paint and paper?" she asked.

Nathan put a clamp on the gasp that wanted to escape.

"No skin off my teeth," Chuck said, "as long as you don't choose any of those bright colors. Don't want to bring down the value of the house." He gave them a knowing look.

Kellie smiled, and Nathan could tell she

was fighting not to speak her mind. "And you're sold on this carpet then?" she asked.

"Well, yeah." Chuck shrugged. "I like it. But there's real hardwoods underneath 'em, if you prefer that kinda thing. Not as comfy on the feet, but I guess they're in pretty good shape."

"I see." Kellie looked around again. "When will the home be available?"

Nathan could hardly believe his ears. She must see something in this place that he didn't.

"I'll be moving midweek," Chuck said. "My daughter and her husband bought one of those fancy houses up in Brenham. They want me to be close. I, uh . . ." He stumbled over his words. "The doc says I've only got about three or four months." His gaze shifted to the ground.

The older man's words almost knocked the wind out of Nathan. "I–I'm so sorry," he stammered. No wonder he'd let the house go. And no wonder he needed to move so quickly.

"Oh, Mr. Henderson." Kellie's eyes filled with tears.

Chuck broke into a broad smile. "Three or four months of chemo, I mean. My daughter wants me to be close to town so I don't have to drive back and forth. I figure

I'll be ready to move back to Greenvine in about six months. Didn't want the house to sit empty all that time."

"It won't be empty." Nathan extended his hand. "We'll take it."

"We will?" Kellie looked up at him with tears still glistening against her lashes. "Are you sure?"

"I'm sure." And with a shake of their hands, they sealed the deal.

CHAPTER 9

Kellie looked around her new home with mixed emotions. The wood-framed house, far cleaner than the day she first saw it, was now filled with brand-new furnishings — at Nathan's request. He'd insisted on pulling up the gold shag carpeting before the furniture went in. She hadn't minded, though the floors underneath needed refinishing.

She glanced at the kitchen. Gone were the old appliances. In their place, Nathan had installed a practical black stove and refrigerator, contemporary in design. He'd insisted these changes were necessary — that this was the only way she would ever feel comfortable — but Kellie wasn't so sure. In fact, she thought the new items looked a bit odd up against the dilapidated structure. She would never hurt Nathan's feelings by sharing this thought, though, not after the trouble he had gone to in order to make things nice for her.

Kellie glanced at her watch. 10:35 a.m. She didn't have time to worry about the house now. It presented far less grief than her current problem — signing onto the Internet. Kellie hadn't counted on the inability to soar across the World Wide Web at the usual rapid pace. Here, away from the city, she had to resort to dial-up. *Dial-up.* She shook her head in disbelief as she sat down in front of the computer.

The disbelief continued as Kellie fought with an uncooperative phone line for an hour and a half. Just about the time she signed on, she would get knocked off again. And today of all days! She'd been advised by a client to purchase a specific number of shares of stock at a current reduced rate. Unfortunately the ups and downs of the market made that transaction impossible, at least without reliable Internet access.

Kellie gave up as the clock struck twelve. She'd lost the opportunity to make the purchase, and nothing could be done about it. With the phone in one hand and laptop in the other, she placed the call to the client and prayed the loss wouldn't be held against her.

After an aggravating conversation that involved groveling and a plea for another chance, she hung up and plopped on the couch. Kellie rubbed her forehead and leaned back to relax. But she couldn't still her mind. Her thoughts bounced back and forth from stock prices to gas prices — Nathan's latest complaint as he traveled back and forth to Houston — to the cost of the rehab where her father now resided.

Kellie sprang from the couch, her mind suddenly made up. Only one thing could make her feel better about this. She needed to get out of the house for a while. She needed to go to town.

She turned the computer off, grabbed her keys and cell phone, and headed out to the car. As Kellie threw the vehicle into reverse, she began to relax. In less than twenty minutes, she would walk through the door of the Bluebonnet Rehab in Brenham. Her father would be waiting. They would share some smiles, and she would fill him in on the things that happened over the past twenty-four hours, as she had yesterday and the day before.

Kellie reached for the cell phone and pressed Nathan's number. He answered on the very first ring, as she pulled her car out onto the highway.

"Kellie?"

Kellie's heart raced as she heard his voice.

"Hi, baby."

"On your way to see your dad?"

"Yep. How'd you know?"

He chuckled. "I think I have your daily schedule down to a science. Every day at 12:10 p.m., you call me. I was actually sitting here, waiting."

"Really?" She felt her lips curl up a bit as she imagined what he must look like, sitting there waiting.

"Really."

"We've gotten pretty good at this," she said. "Can you believe it's only been a week?"

"Seems like years." His voice suddenly sounded tired.

She fought to change the direction of the conversation. "I'm shocked at how much we've gotten done in such a short time. It's pretty amazing when you think about it."

"Maybe that's why I'm so worn out."

"Well, as soon as you get home tonight, I'm going to pamper you." She smiled as she thought through her plan. "I'm cooking chicken cacciatore."

"My favorite."

"I know." She continued to formulate a plan, one she knew he would appreciate. "And I'm going to pick up a cheesecake while I'm in town."

"In town?" He chuckled. "Brenham is 'in town' now?"

"Yes." She laughed. "Funny how things change. Brenham is now the largest town in my little world. But it seems to have everything we need, so I'm not complaining."

"Well, Houston is looking bigger every day," he said, "and emptier than ever, now that you're not here. I went by the condominium this morning on my way in to pick up some more clothes, and it felt . . . odd. It's not the same without you in it."

"Aw." Kellie's lips curled down in a pout. "I miss you, too, but you know what?"

"What?"

"We're going to have a great evening together. Very relaxed. And after dinner, I'm going to rub those aching shoulders of yours," she said.

"Sounds incredible." Nathan paused a moment to take another call. He returned with an abrupt "Can I call you later? They need me down on the third floor."

"Sure." She kept a steady eye on the road. "I'm almost there anyway. I'll see you tonight, baby."

"Later, gator."

Kellie smiled as she finished the drive. *Lord, You've been so awesome to me. You made a way where there was no way.* In her heart she felt a peace, in spite of the current situation. Something about being here, in the place where she grew up, felt right. She would relish every moment — even if it were for a short time.

She pulled into the rehab facility at twelve thirty and climbed from the car, anxiety mounting. As she entered the lobby of her dad's now-familiar home away from home, she waved at the head nurse. "How are you today, Sharen?"

"Fine, girl. How about you?" The jovial woman with the ever-present jumbo loop earrings greeted her with a hug.

"I'm good." *I really am good.*

Sharen smiled. "Well, I'm glad you're here. Your father's been asking for you all morning."

"He has?"

"His speech is getting better every day," Sharen said. "And that man does love to talk."

Kellie responded with a grin. "My father is a very social man."

"I'd say." Sharen nodded, and her earrings bobbed up and down.

They walked together toward his room. Sharen paused for a moment outside his door. She looked at Kellie intently. "Before you go in, I should tell you one thing."

"What?" Kellie prepared herself, in case the news was bad.

"I caught him crying this morning."

Kellie felt tears well up in her eyes. "Are you sure?"

"Yes." The nurse nodded in sympathy. "I think he was overwhelmed. We were trying to get him dressed for the day, and things weren't going well. We asked him to lift his right arm, and he lifted his left — that sort of thing. I think he was embarrassed and maybe a little confused."

Kellie fought to keep her tears in check. "Is he okay now?"

"Yes. The choir director from your church came by a few minutes later and had him singing a song of some sort."

"He has his singing voice back?" Kellie's hopes rose instantly. Her father had always sung — for as long as she could remember. Maybe the Lord would use that singing to bring him out of this awful situation.

"Well . . ." Sharen shrugged. "It was an attempt. At any rate, they were loud. Woke up Mr. Scoggins in the next room, and he had quite a whining session about it."

They giggled together. Kellie then thanked the nurse for the information and braced herself for the usual rush of emotions as she opened the door to her father's room.

"I'm here, Daddy."

He lit up immediately. "K–Kellie."

"How are you today?" She walked to the bed and gave him a hug. His eyes, though full of love, still had a look she couldn't place. *Vacant.* That's what it was. He wasn't quite himself. Not yet anyway.

"F–fine." He sat up, and she plumped his pillows.

Kellie took a seat in the chair next to him and struck up a conversation. Of course she did most of the talking, but her father responded with as many words as he could muster. His eyes spoke the rest. She told him about her morning, about her Internet woes, and her business. She shared what it was like to be back at the church of her childhood and how she felt when she saw Julia and Madison. In short, she talked his ear off.

At one point her father interrupted with one shaky word. "N–Nath–an?"

"Nathan's in Houston, Daddy." Her heart ached, even as she spoke the words. "He's at work today. But he'll be home tonight."

"H–home?"

She reminded him of the rental house in Greenvine and tried to put his mind at ease. Clearly he didn't understand how Nathan could be in one place and she in another.

She rushed past the explanation in the hope that a little would suffice.

"W–where is your m–mother?"

"Ah." *I should have told him right away.* "Mom's at a luncheon at the church today. She'll be here in about an hour."

Her father nodded and smiled. "L–love her."

"I know you love her, Dad." Kellie winked at him. "And she loves you, too."

His eyes filled with tears, and he brushed at them with an undeniable look of anger crossing his face.

Kellie's mind reeled as she contemplated his reaction to her words. Why would that upset him? Of course her mother loved him. After a moment she figured out his thoughts. *He's worried that he's unlovable in this condition. That's what it is.*

She stood and embraced him. "Daddy, you're still the love of her life. That will never change, no matter what."

He nodded, his eyes still moist. "I know." He squeezed her hand and looked directly into her eyes. "L–love you, K–Kell."

"I love you, too, Daddy." She gave him a kiss on the cheek, then sat to chatter awhile longer.

Nathan pulled in the driveway — if one

could call it that — and turned off the car. He sat for a moment, staring at his new home in the dusk. It had an eerie look, one that still made him a little uncomfortable. In some ways the whole experience reminded him of a movie.

"And people think living in the city is scary." He spoke to no one but himself. Of course he had been doing a lot of that lately.

Nathan took the keys out of the ignition and reached for his briefcase. As he climbed from the car, he caught a glimpse of Kellie through the front window. She scurried around the kitchen with her short blond hair in a disheveled mess. He stared in silence as his bride shifted from the stove to the table. She looked — what was the word? — relaxed. She looked relaxed and happy. *Funny.* He'd almost forgotten what that looked like.

Nathan opened the back door of the car and pulled out an overnight bag. With the bag in one hand and briefcase in the other, he crossed the overgrown lawn. Sooner or later he would get to it. Probably later rather than sooner. Nathan entered the house with a rehearsed smile on his face. He didn't want Kellie to see the exhaustion or any hint of frustration. She had been through enough.

She greeted him with a warm hug and a brush of light kisses along his cheek. "How was the drive?"

Nathan fought the temptation to say *long*. He opted, instead, to go another route. After all, the Lord had given him plenty of time to make calls while on the road. And his prayer time had increased, to be sure. Besides, it was a pretty drive, especially in the springtime with the bluebonnets to keep him occupied.

Nathan smiled as he said, "Not bad. I've been listening to tapes from that conference in Austin. I actually made it through the first two."

"Great." She took the briefcase from his hand and set it aside. Her lips turned down in a bit of a pout as she continued. "I had a little trouble signing onto the Internet today, but I called the phone company. They're going to send someone out tomorrow to look at our line."

He had worried about this. In her line of work, an instant connection was critical. "Any consequences?" He almost dreaded her answer.

"Yes." Her gaze shifted downward. "But nothing a little pleading couldn't take care of." She sighed.

He shook his head. "I'm sorry, honey."

"C'est la vie." She gave a wave of her hand, as if to dismiss the whole thing.

Nathan wasn't ready to let go of his troubling thoughts. "What are they saying at the office? Are they okay with this change in plans?"

"So far, so good," she said. "I'm thankful for that."

Nathan breathed a sigh of relief. "Well then, I'll pray the phone company gets the kinks worked out. Looks as if the Lord's already taken care of the rest."

"Yep." She ushered him toward the table. "Hungry, I hope?"

"Starving." He'd barely had time for lunch. Somewhere between the two drives and the workload, he hadn't found time for food today.

She pointed at the dish of chicken cacciatore and the salad and beamed. "I've been working hard."

"I can see that. It looks great." Nathan sat at the unfamiliar table in an unfamiliar chair and ate off an unfamiliar plate. All the while, Kellie chattered merrily. She never picked up on his discomfort, and he never gave her any reason to. He took big bites and listened as she told him about her day. Had she always been this talkative? For some reason he couldn't remember this much gabbing after work. Then again, in the city she had people to talk to all day. Here . . .

Well, here things were different. *Clearly.*

"I went to see my dad." Joy laced her words. "I think he's doing a little better." She paused, and her lashes dampened with tears. "You should see him, Nathan. His face lights up every time I come in the room. The doctor says he'll be up to walking outside by next week. I can't wait. I hope the weather cooperates. I checked the weather report today, and we're supposed to have a lot of rain in the next ten days."

"You checked the weather report?" He didn't recall her ever doing that before.

"Well," she explained, "I read the paper up at the rehab. I've been doing a lot of reading lately."

"Wow." Nathan smiled at her enthusiasm. *I haven't seen this side of her in a long, long time.* Somehow, seeing her so relaxed helped relax him, too.

He decided then and there that he could handle the drives, the loss in income, and the bills from the new house and furnishings — as long as he could look at her peaceful face every night.

CHAPTER 10

Kellie stopped at the grocery store in Greenvine on the way home from visiting her father. She entered the store with the list of needed items in one hand and the cell phone pressed to her ear. She continued an ongoing conversation with Nathan, one that had started twenty minutes prior, as she pulled out of Brenham.

"How late will you be?" Kellie spoke into the phone as she grabbed a shopping cart and headed it toward the produce aisle. One of the wheels didn't seem to be working properly so she switched out one cart for another. Unfortunately, the next one appeared to have the same problem. *Oh well.*

"From what I've been told, this meeting could go on until seven or eight," Nathan explained. "Looks like I'm not going to make it home till ten or after."

She paused long enough to pout. "No way."

"Way."

"Man." Kellie tossed a head of lettuce into her shopping cart and sighed. "I had planned a great dinner. King Ranch Chicken and a brand-new taco-salad recipe I found in a magazine up at the rehab." Her father seemed to spend more time dozing than awake, so she'd had ample time to browse the facility's worn selection of women's magazines. She'd discovered recipes, developed a desire to redecorate, and even come under conviction to intensify her romantic life. Amazing what a few words of encouragement could do.

"I'll still eat when I get in," he said. "But don't wait on me, okay? Go ahead and do your own thing."

Do my own thing? "Are you sure?"

"Yeah. And don't stress so much over the cooking. You're going to make me fat." He chuckled, but Kellie didn't join in the fun. She had grown to love preparing a home-made meal each night, and as thin as Nathan was, she could scarcely imagine him growing plump. In spite of her new recipes.

Nathan let out a groan. "Great. That's my other line. I have to run."

"I miss you, Nathan."

"I miss you, too. See you tonight."

He was gone, and Kellie turned her atten-

123

tion to shopping. Even if he came home late, she wouldn't let that stop her from making a meal he would enjoy. She would continue to do everything she could to let him know how much she appreciated him.

She pushed the cart along, broken wheel bouncing with a *clack, clack, clack.* She glanced to her right and left, still adjusting to the outdated grocery store. It in no way compared to the contemporary, well-stocked markets back home in Houston. To start, it was a fraction of the size. And it offered little variety. In particular this tiny store carried very few of the natural, organic fruits and vegetables she had grown to love.

Well, no bother. *The next time I'm in Houston, I'll go to the whole foods market.* In the meantime, this would have to do. She sorted through the bell peppers, finally choosing two she could tolerate. Next she headed to the tomatoes. She picked her way through the limited selection, bagging three small ones and placing them in the front of her basket next to the peppers.

Kellie rounded the corner onto the bread aisle. She reached for a loaf of bread and placed it in the basket. As she did, a familiar voice caught her attention.

"I have a great recipe for homemade bread."

Kellie looked up into her friend's eyes. "Julia!" she squealed. "I can't believe it."

"Why not?" Julia smiled. "In a town this size, we run into each other all the time. Better get used to it."

"I guess so." Kellie paused as she thought about it. "It's kind of nice. Doesn't happen much in the big city."

Julia quieted Madison, who'd started to squirm in the front of her basket. "This little girl's sleepy. She missed her nap today. We had a tea party for preschool girls up at the civic center. That's why she's so dressed up."

"Well, she looks adorable," Kellie acknowledged. In fact, Madison looked like the cutest thing she had ever seen with her ruffled dress and patent leather shoes. "And it sounds like a lot of fun."

"I'm the activities director for the center," Julia explained. "We do everything from inviting in speakers to taking road trips together. It's a blast."

"Wow." Kellie pondered her friend's excitement. *How can anyone muster that kind of enthusiasm for a children's tea party?*

Julia continued to tend to Madison, who clearly wanted out of the basket. "So, are you getting settled in?" she asked, as she reached to scoop the rambunctious little girl into her arms.

Kellie nodded. "Getting there. The house still needs a lot of work." She and Nathan had spent a great deal of time on the place already, but it would take months to transform the little house into a comfortable living space. Not that they had months.

"Frankie and I bought a little fixer-upper a couple of years ago," Julia said. "It's been a challenge, but we've learned a lot about ourselves along the way. We've done a ton of work on the house — everything from remodeling the kitchen to laying down a wood floor. And I've developed an addiction to home improvement TV in the process." She flashed Kellie a broad smile. "You name it; I watch it. Design shows, landscaping shows, even those funny surprise makeover shows. I love them all."

It looked as if Julia's enthusiasm wasn't limited to her daughter's social life. Kellie couldn't help but wonder about her friend's lifestyle. Did Julia spend her days as full-time mom and activities director and part-time home decorator? Whatever she did with her time, it certainly brought her joy.

"I'd love to come by and see the house sometime," Kellie said. "And you, too, of course. When are you free?"

"I'm pretty open in the afternoons," Julia said. "I'm still teaching art classes at the junior high in the morning. They were great to work around my schedule."

"Oh!" Kellie nearly squealed again. "You're an art teacher. I'd almost forgotten. I sure could use your help choosing paint colors for the house."

"I'd love that." Julia bounced Madison up and down on her hip. "When do you want to get started?"

"The sooner the better."

The two plunged into a lengthy discussion about paint chips and name brands. They contemplated color choices and textures. They debated faux finishes and wallpaper. In short, they had a grand time talking about the what-ifs of home decorating.

After a while, Kellie changed the direction of their conversation. She had been wondering about Julia's husband for some time now and couldn't wait to ask about him.

"What's Frankie like?"

"Oh, he's awesome." Julia's face lit up. "He's got the most amazing sense of humor. He keeps me laughing all the time."

"What sort of work does he do?"

"He's a mechanic. He works at Clayton's Automotive up on 290. You've probably been by it a hundred times."

"Oh, I think I've seen that place."

"I met him when my alternator went out."

Julia chuckled. "We've always said the Lord brought us together. Only problem with that theory is it cost me about three hundred dollars to have the crazy thing fixed."

Kellie smiled.

Julia continued with great enthusiasm. "But you should see him with Madison. They're the perfect father-daughter team. And he treats me like such a queen. He does most of the cooking — not because he doesn't like mine, but because he enjoys doing it. He might not be the most handsome man" — she paused for a moment and seemed to disappear into her thoughts — "and we'll probably never live in a really nice home or anything like that. But he's the man of my dreams, no doubt. God knew what He was doing."

Kellie looked at her friend with newfound admiration. "Well, he sounds great. And I can't wait to get to know him better." A thought suddenly came to her, one she could not let go of. "You know, I think Nathan could use some friends from the area. He's private, but I can tell he gets a little lonely sometimes. Maybe you and Frankie could come over sometime for dinner. Maybe we could watch a movie or something after."

"Sounds like fun." Julia's brow wrinkled

as she continued. "But I'd have to bring the baby. Would that be okay?"

Kellie reached to play with Madison's curls once again. "I wouldn't have it any other way."

Madison began to fuss a bit, and Julia placed her back in the front of the basket. "I guess I'd better get this little girl home," she said with a sigh. "Her daddy's going to be arriving any minute now."

Daddy. As soon as the word flitted through her mind, Kellie's eyes watered. *Lord, please heal my dad. And, Lord — give Nathan the desire to be a dad.*

Where the words came from, she had no idea.

Nathan awoke early Saturday morning. He glanced at the clock. 5:55. *Why can't I ever sleep past six?*

He knew the answer. His body had grown accustomed to the early morning hours. But on Saturday? Surely on the weekend, he could catch a few more winks.

The first hint of sunlight peeked in through the window. Nathan closed his eyes to shut it out. Unfortunately nothing could drown out the noise of birds chirping in the tree outside their bedroom window. He would never grow used to it, not if he lived here a hundred years. He yearned for the noises of the city — the sound of cars racing by, horns honking, tires squealing, people hollering back and forth. He strained to hear those wonderful, familiar sounds.

Nothing. Only the irritating hum of crickets and the wind blowing through the trees. How did people live like this? Nathan rolled back over and punched the pillow. *I'm going to sleep if it kills me.* He lay in silence for a few minutes, willing himself into a slumber. Kellie's gentle breathing almost made him envious. *Am I jealous of my wife?*

He drew in a deep breath as he pondered the thought. He had been more than a little envious of her over the past couple of weeks, though he hadn't admitted it to anyone. Even himself. But how could he not feel some small degree of resentment? It must be nice to be able to sleep in every day, then wake up to a quiet home. No people shouting orders, racing up and down hallways, pressing into elevators. No looming deadlines or irritable coworkers.

He punched the pillow again. *Be fair, man. She's working from home. It's not as if she doesn't have a job. And even if she didn't —*

The concept hit him like a meteor plunging from the sky. What if she didn't? What if Kellie turned out to be one of those women who simply wanted to stay home and raise babies? Would that be so awful? He swallowed hard, thinking about it. Sure, it interrupted their well-conceived plan, but what if God had a different plan in mind all along?

Nathan lay silently as he pondered the thought. *We'll have children one of these days, and they'll have everything we can afford to give them. They'll go to the best schools. They'll get the best possible care from a private nanny, if need be. At any rate, they'll be well taken care of.*

Well taken care of. He looked over at Kellie once more. Her back rose and fell with each breath. Nathan noticed how she'd changed over the past few weeks. He saw a peace in her that he hadn't sensed before. She'd lost the frenzied, worried look that so often etched her eyes. In its place, a bright-eyed, well-rested woman greeted him each night as he entered the house. With a tasty meal on the table, to boot.

"She's well taken care of now." He whispered the words, then sat up in the bed to look at her more pensively. Here, in this place, she appeared to be thriving. The only thing missing from her life was — well, to be honest — him.

But there's nothing I can do about that. It's

not my fault. He wrestled with the Lord a few moments over the issue. How could he handle so much at once — a mortgage, rent, bills, the commute — and still give her the things she needed? Surely he had shown Kellie in a dozen different ways how much he loved her, even if he couldn't give her the time she needed.

Nathan thought back over the gifts he'd given Kellie over the past three years. Gifts to make up for not being there as much as he should. Gifts to bring a smile to her face. Gifts to replace the one thing she wanted.

Time. All she needed was time with him. That's all she'd ever needed or wanted. *She's about quality time. That's how she wants me to show her love. But how, Lord? How do I do that when I have no time?*

Then again, he had time right now. Nathan reached over and ran his finger across Kellie's cheek.

She awoke with a start. "Nathan, is everything okay?"

"I'm sorry." He pulled his hand back, repentant. "I didn't mean to wake you." He drew closer to her and kissed her on the cheek. "Unless you want to be awake, that is."

"What time is it?" She looked at the clock and groaned. "Whoa."

"We can sleep awhile longer." He leaned back against the pillow and yawned.

"Okay." She rolled over and leaned her head against his chest. About the time he thought she'd fallen asleep again, she reached to plant a tiny kiss on his shoulder. Nathan responded by wrapping her in his arms.

CHAPTER 11

Kellie nudged Nathan with her elbow more than once during Pastor Jamison's sermon the following Sunday. She didn't see how anyone could doze through such a life-changing message. How long had it been since she'd heard the gospel preached with such clarity? And how long had it been since she'd found herself in such a peaceful setting to take it in?

She glanced around the room, still listening. The same organ sat to the left of the stage, the grand piano to the right. She'd played that piano as a child with her sister Katie singing along.

And that pulpit. How many sermons had she heard from behind that hand-carved wooden pulpit? How many times had Pastor Jamison given a call for people to come forward for prayer? And how many times had she found herself at the altar, weeping? Those memories faded into one clear reality. This room held a host of memories — all wonderful. In this place, she had given her heart to the Lord. In this place she had come to understand His call on her life. And now in this place, she sat with her husband at her side, content.

Kellie continued to look around the room as she listened to the pastor's words. The stained glass windows caught her eye. Each was unique to itself, perhaps not as brilliant as those in the city churches but with every bit as much meaning. Perhaps more. Her gaze came to rest on one in particular — Jesus making His way up the hill toward Calvary. Sunlight from the outside brought the colors to light. Each red and blue seemed more brilliant than she'd remembered.

Though Kellie couldn't read the inscription from where she sat, she knew from memory what it said: IN LOVING MEMORY OF KENTON CONWAY SR. — her grandfather — one of the founding members of this church. She remembered his laugh and the way his breath always smelled of mint. She remembered his silver hair, sculpted in place with slick hair gel. But more than anything, she remembered that eventful Sunday during her seventh-grade year — a few short months after he'd passed away.

Pastor Jamison had dedicated the colorful window with tears in his eyes. In fact, everyone in the place had damp eyes.

Just as she did now. But the window stirred other feelings now — feelings she couldn't seem to control. Staring at the window made her think of her father and brought a sense of sadness. She pushed it aside and focused on Pastor Jamison.

Of course it was a little difficult, with Nathan dozing off to her left. Every five or six minutes, his breathing changed, grew heavier. Then, about the time she found herself captivated by the message, he would let out the tiniest bit of a snore. The little girl in the pew in front of them seemed to find it amusing. The darling youngster turned around on several occasions and made funny faces. Kellie tried to stay focused but found it difficult. She was thankful her mother was off in children's church. She was the sort to find this funny, too. Kellie found the whole thing more difficult.

On the other hand, she reasoned as she jabbed her elbow into his side for the umpteenth time, *it's not as if he's getting enough sleep. He's wearing himself out driving back and forth so I can be here. He's making all the sacrifices, and I —*

She pursed her lips as she contemplated what Nathan must think of her. *Does he think I'm lazy? Does he think I don't care about his workload? I do care.* But had he misinterpreted her motives? Had she in some small way let her love for her father seem more important than her love for her husband?

Kellie gave a little shiver as the thought sank in. She tried to stay focused as the pastor wrapped up the message but couldn't seem to let go of the thought that Nathan must be harboring some internal frustrations he wasn't voicing. Perhaps they would have a good, long conversation about it. *This afternoon.*

As the service drew to a close, Nathan seemed to be more himself. He sang reverently, with his eyes shut, during the invitation and stood in silent prayer for those who responded. He clutched her hand and eased her along through the crowd toward the back of the sanctuary as the service was dismissed. They encountered more than one interruption along the way.

"Kellie, where is your mother this morning?" Mrs. Dennison asked. "I didn't see her."

"Oh, this is her week to teach children's church," Kellie explained. "She wouldn't miss that for the world."

"I should've known." The older woman opened her arms for a warm embrace. "She's such a worker bee."

"Yes, she is."

Kellie willingly allowed herself to be hugged, then turned back toward Nathan, worried he had grown bored and wanted to escape. Instead, she found him involved in an easy conversation with Hal O'Keefe. She caught the tail end of Hal's story — something about a fishing trip he planned to take the following week. Was he — no, surely he couldn't be inviting Nathan. Nathan had never fished a day in his life.

When the words, "I'd love to, sir," slipped from her husband's lips, Kellie thought perhaps the time had come to get her ears checked.

Hal slapped him on the back before heading off into a conversation with one of the deacons.

"You didn't have to do that," she whispered into Nathan's ear as they made their way into the lobby. "I'm sure his feelings wouldn't have been hurt."

Nathan's lips turned down into a frown, and his wrinkled forehead spoke volumes. "But I want to go fishing. I never get a chance to do stuff like that."

"You do?" She stared up at him with a broad smile as relief swept through her. "I thought you were afraid you'd hurt his feelings, that you were scared to say no to him."

"Do you think I have trouble saying no to people?" His question was almost accusing.

Only to me. She shook her head, frustrated. "No, Nathan, I don't. And I'm excited you want to go fishing with Hal. I just didn't want you to feel obligated."

He shrugged. "Sounds like fun, actually. And it's not as if I won't be up at five thirty next Saturday anyway. You know me."

Yes. She knew him, and that's what worried her. He hadn't rested in weeks. But perhaps next Saturday's trip to the river with Hal would give him a chance not only to connect with a wonderful man of God but also to get some well-deserved rest. With a pole in his hand.

Kellie squeezed his fingers as a sign of approval, and they took a few steps into the crowded lobby. She quickly found herself engaged in a conversation with Julia, who'd appeared with Madison in tow. Frankie, ever his wife's social equal, gabbed at length with one of his friends off to her left.

"A bunch of us are going up to the cafeteria on the highway for lunch," Julia explained. "I thought you two might like to

139

join us. And your mom, too, of course." She bounced Madison up and down on her hip as she spoke.

"Oh, it sounds . . ." Kellie hesitated before responding. How would Nathan feel about eating in a cafeteria with a mob of church friends? She looked up into his eyes for her answer.

"Sounds great to me," he said. "If you think we've got time."

Kellie glanced at her watch. 12:15. "Dad's not expecting us till two. Surely we'll be done by then. And maybe" — she smiled at the thought — "maybe we can take him a plate of food — offer him something different for a change." She nodded in Julia's direction. "We'd love to meet you."

"So you're coming with us?" Frankie turned to join them with a broad smile. He scooped Madison into his arms, and she let out a squeal as he lifted her into the air above his head.

"Frankie, don't do that." Julia gave him a firm scolding, but he seemed to take it in stride.

"She's not scared," Frankie insisted.

"I know, but . . ."

Kellie smiled as Madison let out another squeal from above the crowd.

"She's a daddy's girl." Frankie lowered

his daughter to his chest and planted a kiss on her forehead.

Julia shook her head, then turned her attention back to Kellie. "Men."

Kellie didn't dare look into Nathan's eyes. She might read too much into his expression. Instead, she took his hand, and they pressed through the crowd into the parking lot.

"Oh, wow." She glanced up at the sky, brilliant blue and as clear as a glass of water. Not a cloud in sight. "It's a gorgeous day. And I can't believe it's this warm."

"It's spring, all right," Nathan said. "I've been watching the bluebonnets up and down 290 as I drive back and forth. I don't remember seeing anything like it before."

"They've always been there," Kellie pondered aloud. "I guess we've never paid that much attention before." Funny how much they hadn't noticed before — like the melodic sound of birds singing outside their bedroom window and the tiny beams of sunlight peeking through the shade first thing in the morning. She loved every bit of it.

"Right." He squeezed her hand, and they walked a few steps in silence.

Several feet from the car, Kellie's mother met up with them. Nathan shared their lunch plans, and she quickly agreed to come along.

"Sounds like fun," she said. "And it's just what Kenton would want me to do."

Kellie found herself smiling all the way to the restaurant. She and Nathan chatted about the service, the people, and the warm reception. He seemed eager to visit with her father today and oddly eager to meet with Hal next Saturday. And something else was different about him, too, though Kellie couldn't put her finger on it.

Nathan seemed . . . relaxed. Yes, that's what it was. In all the years she'd known him, she had rarely seen this side of him.

But what she saw, she liked.

Nathan sat next to his wife and chatted at length with Frankie about her new car. The fellow, who had first come across as a country bumpkin, seemed knowledgeable about the particular make and model, even commenting on the engine size and gas mileage.

"When you're ready for an oil change, just bring it in to me," Frankie said with an inviting smile.

"Well, we get free oil changes for the first year," Nathan explained with a shrug. "So . . ."

Frankie nodded. "I figured. But you have to take it into the dealership for that, right?"

"Right." *Hadn't thought about that. When could I possibly —*

"Just bring it to me," Frankie said. "I'll take good care of you."

Nathan nodded. "Sounds good. To be honest, it's hard to find a mechanic you can trust —" He started to say "in the city" but held his tongue and let it rest there.

The conversation shifted to the house and the work still undone. Nathan chuckled as Kellie described, with some sense of drama, their first visit to the place. Her eyes grew large as she told everyone at the table about poor Mr. Henderson and his dilapidated home. But those same eyes brimmed over with tears when she reached the part about his cancer treatments. The whole table grew eerily silent.

"We'll add him to our prayer list," Julia said. "We have a great prayer chain up at the church."

"Prayer chain?" Nathan asked.

His mother-in-law piped in, "When there's a need in the church, they let Mrs. Dennison know, and she makes a call to the next person on the prayer chain. They pray together aloud over the phone, and then that person calls the next one on the list.

And on it goes."

"Ah."

Julia nodded. "We've seen so many miracles on our little prayer chain." She reached to squeeze Kellie's hand. "And I just know your dad is going to be one of them."

Kellie gripped his fingers and gave him a smile of contentment. For some time, Nathan sat like that — with her hand firmly clasped in his own — tuning out the conversations around him. He wanted to stay focused, wanted to join in more, but something else drew his attention away at the moment.

Hal O'Keefe. His father-in-law's good buddy and his soon-to-be fishing partner. Nathan had his suspicions about why Hal wanted to spend a little private time with him. The good-natured older fellow had telephoned a few days prior with news that he'd hoped would stay quiet on Nathan's end.

The city of Greenvine was in trouble. Financial trouble. And Kenton, for years the city's dutiful comptroller, remained blissfully unaware in his current condition.

"I thought you might be willing to give us some advice," Hal had said over the phone. "Not trying to get you too involved. But

144

since Kenton's in rehab and can't take care of this personally, the rest of us are clueless. We need someone with your expertise."

For once Nathan was glad his father-in-law wasn't fully aware of the goings-on around him. Knowing Kenton the way he did, he'd want to be back up at the office, fixing things.

But fixing things this time might take some doing.

Nathan pondered the situation a few minutes, trying to decide how involved he should get. *My plate is so full already. I don't have time to think about taking on much more.*

A shock wave of laughter brought him back to the present. Julia's little girl had strings of spaghetti hanging from her hair. Her tiny bulb of a nose was covered in red sauce, and she grinned like a Cheshire cat.

Nathan looked over at Kellie, who laughed so hard her face turned red.

She faced him head-on with a cockeyed grin. "Isn't that the funniest thing you've ever seen?"

He answered with the most serious face he could muster. "Nope."

"It's not?" Her lips turned down a bit.

"This is." Nathan reached to pull a string of spaghetti out of her hair and placed it on the table in front of her for all to see.

Kellie gasped, and her hands shot up to her hair to search for more. Finally convinced she was pasta-free, she turned back to the group with cheeks ablaze. "Why didn't someone say something?"

Everyone began to laugh and talk at once. Nathan pushed aside thoughts of the city's financial woes and turned his attention, instead, to the beautiful woman at his side.

CHAPTER 12

Kellie sailed through the following week, shocked at the passage of time. With each new day, her father's condition improved, though ever so slightly. With each new day, she also faced work-related challenges and countless phone calls from her office in Houston. Every few minutes, she questioned their decision to be here — in Greenvine. Every few minutes, she wondered how — or if — she would ever be able to leave.

On Thursday afternoon, after visiting her father, Kellie went by the civic center to meet with Julia and the children. All the way there she praised God for the news. Her father had taken giant leaps forward over the past week. Just this afternoon he had eaten on his own. Held the fork in his hand and taken real bites. He was also starting to speak in clear, coherent sentences. Almost clear anyway. And he'd taken several steps with the aid of a walker yesterday and seemed to be responding to the daily dose of physical therapy.

Kellie could hardly wait to tell Julia. She knew her best friend would praise God alongside her.

She walked in on a bustle of activity and shared her news. As expected, Julia let out a loud "Praise the Lord" and lifted her hand in praise toward the sky. Kellie smiled. Clearly her friend was enthusiastic about more than home improvement. Her love of the Lord was evident in all she said and did.

Kellie looked down at the room full of exuberant youngsters. They sat at a table loaded with craft items. Colorful beads, sequins, and feathers filled the center of the table.

"We're making drama masks," Julia explained as she placed a bright red and purple sequined mask in front of her face. The lips curled up in a smile. "This one's comedy." She spoke in a happy voice. She replaced it with a black and gold one with lips turned down. "This one's tragedy." She spoke in a somber voice.

Kellie clasped her hands together, ready to join the fun. "Cool. Sounds like a blast. Can I make one?"

"Of course!" Julia shoved several supplies her way and gestured to a seat.

Kellie sat down and joined the fun. The children laughed at length as the project consumed them. On more than one occasion, Kellie sprang to rescue some little one from near disaster. She soon became absorbed in their stories as she worked alongside them.

"You've worked with kids before," Julia observed.

"Um . . . not really."

Julia's face reflected her surprise. "Well, you're a natural at it."

Kellie pondered her friend's words. She'd never considered herself a natural at anything — except numbers.

Wow. I hope that's not my legacy. Won't look very good on my tombstone. "SHE WAS GREAT WITH NUMBERS."

Kellie pushed aside the nagging thought and tried to stay focused. As the children busied themselves, Julia whispered a few quiet words on a subject that startled her a bit.

"I guess you've heard —"

"About?" Kellie looked over at her friend, puzzled.

Julia looked around to make sure they weren't being overheard. "The trouble."

"Trouble?" Kellie thought of the church, and her heart quickened. "No, I haven't heard anything. What's happened?"

Julia pursed her lips. "We found out a couple of days ago. Frankie's dad is mayor now — did you know?"

Kellie's mouth flew open. "I've been so focused on everything else that I didn't make the connection. I'm sorry."

"Oh, don't be." Julia shrugged. "It's just that we hear a lot of what's going on with the city before some of the others."

"The trouble has to do with Greenvine?" Kellie set her mask down on the table so she could concentrate.

"Yes." Julia drew in a deep breath. "It's something pretty big, too. I don't understand the technical lingo. Something about arbitraged . . ." She bit her lip, clearly trying to remember the rest.

"Arbitraged bonds?" Kellie asked.

Julia shrugged. "I think that's right. Something about a bad investment."

Kellie's heart felt as if it would hit the floor. "Or a bad *investor*," she was quick to add. "Someone scammed the city leaders?"

"Pretty much."

Julia turned her attention to one of the little girls who needed help, and Kellie pondered her friend's words.

"Daddy." She whispered the word, suddenly aware of the truth. Her father had apparently put his trust — and ultimately the city's trust — into the hands of someone who'd proven him wrong. And he didn't even know it.

Kellie put together a plan in her mind. She would find out the *who*s, *what*s, and *when*s and would get to work. But she would need help. She would need —

Nathan.

She would need Nathan. Where her knowledge ended, his began. Together they could work as a team to help Greenvine reclaim what it had lost. Together they could —

She stopped herself in the middle of the thought. *I can't do that to him. He's overwhelmed with work already. He hardly has time enough for —*

Kellie struggled with the next thought. Nathan hadn't had much time for her lately, but she certainly couldn't blame him for that. Not with the house in such a state of disrepair and the drive back and forth to Houston.

And something else seemed to be missing from his life, as well. His passion for God seemed to be — what was the word? *Waning.* She didn't see him reading his Bible much these days, and it had been ages since they'd had one of their famous "let's talk about how we're doing spiritually" conversations. He always initiated those.

But not now. Now he was just too busy. So how could she ask more of him?

Kellie squirmed in her chair, thinking. She ached for Nathan. She missed him, maybe more than she had ever missed him back in Houston. This was a different kind of missing — the kind that created a tight grip around her heart and wouldn't let go.

Lord, I have to give this situation over to You. I don't know what else to do with it.

She and Nathan would get through this season, she felt sure. She loved him with a passion that seemed to exceed any fears or frustrations. Yes, her love had changed over the years. This was a different, more committed kind of love — of the "in it for the long haul" variety.

Her relationship with Nathan was key.

On the other hand, she loved Greenvine and wanted to do what she could to help. She would try, at any rate. She would make her father proud. And when he was on his feet again, he would get back to work, doing what he loved best. Somehow, she would manage to do it all.

"Earth to Kellie."

She looked up into Julia's laughing eyes. "Hey."

"Hey to you, too." Her friend reached to pat her on the back. "Thought we'd lost you there for a minute."

"No, I'm still here." Even as she spoke the words, Kellie understood their depth. She was still here — in Greenvine.

And here she wanted to stay.

Nathan sat at lunch with his boss in a crowded downtown restaurant. All around him people hollered out conversations to one another above the din of clinking silverware. Busboys loaded their trays, and waiters took orders. The whole place was abuzz with activity, and he loved every bit of it.

Mr. Abernathy looked him in the eye. "Nathan, I've wanted to talk with you awhile now. I'm proud of the work you've accomplished at Siefert and Collins."

"Thank you, sir." Nathan took a sip of tea and tried to relax. Something about these one-on-one meetings with his boss still made him a little nervous.

"There's just one thing." The older man looked at him intently.

"Sir?"

"Well." Mr. Abernathy stared him down as he spoke. "You haven't exactly been yourself lately. You seem distracted, to be honest."

"Ah." Nathan should've been prepared for those words but wasn't. "I, um . . ." No point in arguing about it, especially when it was true.

The older man gave him a sympathetic look. "I know you've been through a lot in recent weeks. And I know you're torn between two places right now."

"Yes, sir. But I've tried hard not to let that interfere with my work."

"It's not your work that's suffering necessarily," Mr. Abernathy explained. "I'm more concerned about your health."

"My health?"

A look of genuine concern filled his boss's eyes. "You seem worn out most of the time, and that concerns me. Are you getting enough sleep?"

Nathan sighed. "I'm trying. It's an adjustment. And the drive . . ." The drive was wearing on him. What had begun as a great opportunity to spend more time in prayer had turned into a daily battle with his own internal thoughts. Many times he had all but pressed God out of the conversation altogether. Without meaning to, of course.

"Have you given any thought to staying at your condominium a few nights during the week?" Mr. Abernathy's words brought

Nathan back from his ponderings.

"Yes. In fact, I plan to stay in town tonight. I've got too much on my plate to drive home."

"Home?" The word sounded more like an accusation.

Why did I say home? I didn't mean home. I meant Greenvine.

"Well, Greenvine is more of a home away from home." Nathan braved a smile, hoping to bring assurance. "It's certainly not the kind of home I've planned for my family and myself."

"Of course not." Mr. Abernathy's eyes narrowed. "I know better than that. You fit right in here in the city. Always have."

Nathan thought about those words as they finished their lunch. He'd been born and raised in Houston and had never planned to leave. His parents were here. His job was here.

His home was here.

CHAPTER 13

The following Sunday morning, Nathan had a hard time waking up. He'd spent the better part of the night tossing and turning. He couldn't seem to still his mind. Problems at work, coupled with his concerns over Hal's revelations during their fishing trip, kept his mind occupied

He glanced at the clock several times during the night. 2:15, 4:36, 5:44. He must have rested somewhere between those times, but he sure didn't feel like it when the alarm went off at seven. And then there was that ever-present aggravation of birds shrieking outside his window. There weren't enough pillows in the world to drown out that nuisance.

Kellie rolled out of bed with her usual ease. She gave him a soft kiss on the cheek and headed to the bathroom to brush her teeth. He would join her in a minute. Right now he had more important things to take care of.

At 7:20, Kellie eased him back away with her gentle words. "Getting up, sleepyhead? I've already had my shower." She leaned down to kiss him on the forehead.

"Uh-huh." His head felt heavy against the pillow. For some reason, he couldn't seem to budge. *Just a few more minutes won't hurt.*

She awoke him again at 7:55, a look of concern on her face. "Are you sick, Nathan?" This time she didn't sound quite as gentle.

He tried to focus on her words but couldn't keep his eyes open long enough. "I–I'm fine."

She stared at him with a degree of concern registering in her eyes. "You never sleep this late. I already have my makeup on, and breakfast is getting cold."

"Okay." He sat up slowly, then leaned back against the headboard. "I don't know what's wrong with me."

She gave him an encouraging nod. "I'm sure you'll be fine after your shower."

Kellie padded off into the kitchen, and Nathan allowed the weight of his eyelids to pull them down, down, down once more.

It seemed like only a second more, and Kellie shouted in his ear. "Nathan, what's going on?" He wiped the drool from the edge of his lip and shot a glance at the clock. 8:37. She stood before him, fully dressed, purse slung over her shoulder, Bible in her hand. Clearly ready to leave. And clearly in a bad frame of mind.

"I–I'm coming." He swung his legs over the side of the bed and stretched. But how could he leave when his head felt heavier than a bucket of lead?

"I don't see the point." She pursed her lips and crossed her arms at her chest.

"Are you mad at me?"

"Not mad." Her eyes reflected a strange sadness. "I know you're tired."

"It's not just that," he tried to explain. "I couldn't sleep at all last night. There's too much going on in my head. And speaking of which" — he rubbed his aching head, willing the dull ache to go away — "my head is killing me."

Kellie's expression softened, and she let her arms fall to her sides. "I'm sorry, baby. Do you need something for the pain?"

He nodded, and she went to the medicine cabinet in search of the pills. When she returned to his bedside with a glass of water in one hand and medicine in the other, he offered up a smile. "Thanks for taking care of me."

"Wish I could do more." She glanced at her watch. "But I need to go. It's getting late, and I don't want to miss Sunday school. I'm supposed to be reporting on my dad's condition. He's doing so much better, and I can't wait to tell them."

"I know, Kellie." Nathan stood to give her a kiss. "And I'm sorry I'm going to miss it. I wish I could be there."

"I'll see you afterward," she said. "But it's going to be later than usual. We have that fund-raiser dinner for the missions trip the teens are taking to Nicaragua this summer. I promised I'd help with the slave auction. I'm handling the money part of it."

"Man." Nathan paused to think. "I forgot about that. I told some kid I might buy his time. Maybe get him to come and do some work on our yard." How could he have forgotten when their overgrown yard beckoned?

"That was Jerry Chandler," she reminded him. "But I'll explain you're not feeling well." Kellie walked toward the bedroom door, then turned back to look at him. "I could still arrange for him to come and work on the yard next Saturday, if you like. Might cost a little more than we'd pay otherwise, but it's for a good cause."

Good girl, Kellie. I knew I could count on

you to take care of that for me. "That's fine. Whatever you think is best."

"Okay." She paused for one last time. "I should mention that I'll be at rehab from two until about four or so. If you want to join me —"

"I'll be there." He sat back down on the edge of the bed. "I promise."

"Okay. Well . . ." She turned and walked from the room. He heard the front door slam as his head hit the pillow.

Can I help it if I'm worn out? Can I help it if my head is killing me?

Nathan pouted in silence. He didn't want to get up. He didn't want to face a church full of carefree, smiling people. Not today.

No, today he wanted to lie right here, snoring peacefully. The world could go on spinning without him for a while longer. Kellie could —

He punched the pillow and fought to get comfortable. Kellie could surely face her friends and family without him this once. After all, it wasn't as if she'd been the one working 24/7. What more could she expect?

And of course he'd be there to see her father at two. What kind of person did she think he was? An internal argument began, one he couldn't seem to squelch. It wasn't as if she'd spent any time with his family

160

over the past month. Or that she'd spent a lot of time talking to him about his struggles, his thoughts, his concerns.

Nathan rubbed at his aching head and tried to still the frustrations that had erupted from out of nowhere. *Lord, I don't know where this is coming from. I had no clue I was this bugged about things.*

"I'm just tired." He spoke aloud to the empty room then let out an exaggerated yawn. "That's all that's wrong with me."

Nathan thought about his work back in Houston. The company seemed to be going in a thousand different directions at once. He had hoped the meeting with Mr. Abernathy would bring some order to the confusion in his mind, but things had only grown worse. Chaos reigned at Siefert and Collins. And somehow he managed to be stuck in the middle of it. This coming week he'd have to spend at least one or two nights in town to accomplish all that needed to be done. He'd stay at the condo.

The condo. Nathan slapped himself on the head, remembering. He'd received a call on his cell phone on Friday about a problem with the condominium. Something about a leak in the bathroom that had caused flooding for a neighbor downstairs. The maintenance people had stopped the flow of water, but he still needed to hire a plumber to fix the problem.

I'll take care of that first thing tomorrow morning. Right now I need to get some sleep.

He gripped the pillow with both arms and clamped his eyes shut. Sunlight streamed through the cracks in the wood shutters at the window. Outside, a flock of birds continued to chirp in a crazy chorus, nearly driving him out of his mind.

"Why is it so stinkin' noisy in the country?" He rolled over in the other direction and put the pillow over his ear. *And why is Kellie so infatuated with this place?*

He pondered the thought, eyes still squeezed shut. She loved it here. The thought plagued him. At the root of his headache, his frustrations, his pent-up anger lay that one, horrible thought.

Kellie loved it here. And perhaps she always would.

But what could he do about that? How could he counteract it? Something needed to be done — and quickly.

An idea took shape, one that wouldn't leave him alone. She had forgotten what it was like to be in the city. He would take her back to Houston for a couple of days. They'd have a night on the town at that great little French restaurant. They would talk about the condo and their investments. They would start planning that trip to Europe to renew their vows. Everything would be like it was.

Do I want things to be like they were?

He punched the pillow again, sleep a distant dream. Did he want life to return to normal? Wasn't Kellie more peaceful? Didn't he enjoy getting to know the people at church? Wasn't the Lord providing for all their needs?

Nathan groaned, then sat up in the bed. He swung his legs over the side and bowed his head in shame. *Lord, what's wrong with me? What is going on?*

With turmoil still eating at him, Nathan slipped down onto his knees. Enough with all this arguing. What he wanted — what he needed — was time with the Lord.

Kellie cried as she drove along the country road toward town. Frustration moved her to tears, not anger. At least not anger at her husband. At the enemy perhaps.

She didn't blame Nathan for not getting out of bed. She understood his need for rest. She could relate to his exhaustion. She'd lived in an exhausted state for the past three years.

She didn't hold any grudges. He had done

so much for her. She only wished this season would somehow resolve itself so they could have more time together.

With a heavy heart, Kellie continued her drive to the church.

CHAPTER 14

"How does this sign look?" Nathan stretched his arms up as high as he could, lifting the banner above the front door of his in-laws' home.

Kellie clasped her hands over her mouth, then released them triumphantly. "Oh! It looks great."

He scrambled to get the large vinyl banner hung straight. After he was sure he had it up properly, he stepped down from the ladder for a look.

"Welcome home, Kenton." He whispered the words, thrilled at the joy they brought.

"Can you believe it?" Kellie slipped her arm around his waist. "He's coming home." A tear slipped out of the corner of her eye, and she brushed it away with a fingertip. "I'm not sad," she assured him. "Not at all. In fact, I'm so happy I just can't hold the tears back."

"I know, babe." Nathan's heart swelled as

he pressed a kiss on her forehead.

Kellie beamed. "And having Katie here makes everything perfect. I've missed her so much."

"I know your sister is glad to be back," Nathan said.

Kellie glanced at her watch. "We only have ten minutes. Mom called when they left the rehab and said six thirty."

The front door swung open, and Mrs. Dennison stepped outside. "I've got everything ready in the kitchen." She beamed with pride. "Do you need my help out here with anything?"

"I think we have it covered." Nathan folded up the stepladder and carried it to the garage as she headed back inside. Even from here, he could hear the bustle of the crowd in the house. The noise level was at a cheerful high. At least ten or twelve of Kenton's nearest and dearest friends awaited his arrival. They would welcome him home in style — with good food, good conversation, and even a few tears. Nathan could see it all now.

It must be nice to have friends like that, he reasoned. *People who stick with you through thick or thin.*

He had friends, of course — men he played racquetball with, coworkers he'd grown to admire and converse with on a personal level. And then there were the guys he'd grown up with, his buddies from high school. Of course they hadn't seen one another for years. They had no — what was the word? — longevity. They had no longevity. He had temporary friends. Well, near-friends really.

This more intimate type of friendship had somehow eluded him. For a moment Nathan wondered who might be waiting in the living room for him, if he were in Kenton's place.

"Everything okay out here?" Kellie appeared at his side.

"Yes." He pressed the ladder against the wall and turned to pull her into his arms. "I was just thinking."

"About what?" Her face filled with concern immediately, and Nathan knew why. He'd done more than his share of grumbling over the past week. The plumber overcharged him for work at the condo; a tire blew out on his car on the trip back from town Wednesday night; and — to top it all off — Kellie hadn't been able to join him for that in-town romantic getaway he'd planned.

Not that he blamed her. With the excitement surrounding her father's upcoming release, she had been needed here, in Green-vine.

He turned to face her. "I was thinking about how blessed your dad is." Nathan ran the back of his index finger along the edge of Kellie's cheek. She responded by leaning into his chest as he continued. "He has some great friends."

"Yes. They're awesome." She paused, then came alive with her next words. "Oh, speaking of friends, Frankie said to tell you those new wheels you ordered are in. He said they look great. You're going to love them."

"I can't wait." He had happily ordered them at Frankie's suggestion, knowing they would dress up his vehicle.

"Speaking of Frankie, he and Julia are inside with the others. They just got here."

"Great." Nathan smiled and took her hand. They walked in the house arm in arm, then separated to greet the crowd. He grinned as he made the rounds from person to person. There was no lack of conversation — or love — in this room.

When his father-in-law arrived at last, the atmosphere changed immediately. Tears of joy sprang up in nearly every eye, and his friends ushered him in like royalty. After he took his place on the sofa, Kenton looked over the room, his own eyes filled.

"It's . . . it's good to be home."

Nathan felt Kellie's hand tighten in his own.

"We're happy to have you home, Daddy." Kellie sat next to him and planted a tender kiss on his cheek. The sight of Kellie with her father warmed Nathan's heart. When her sister, Katie, joined them on the sofa, the chattering began in earnest.

The room became lively again as people made their way over to the couch, one by one. They offered warm words, prayers, encouragement, and even a laugh or two. Nathan watched it all from a careful distance — close enough to let Kellie know he wasn't going anywhere, far enough away to give her the space she needed with her dad.

Hal prayed for the food, and everyone loaded their paper plates, chatted merrily, and ate with abandon. Nathan filled a plate with meatballs, some little sausages, cheese and crackers, and an assortment of fresh veggies with dip. He'd come back for dessert later.

On second thought. He reached to grab two peanut butter cookies and a piece of cheesecake while they were still there to grab. In this kind of crowd, what he wanted might not still be there when he got back.

Balancing the plate in one hand, Nathan

popped a piece of cheese into his mouth.

Hal slapped him on the back, nearly sending the piece of cheese down his throat. "Getting enough to eat?"

Nathan nodded, then reached to pick up a paper cup from a stack on the table.

"Here, let me get that for you." Hal took the cup. "What did you want in it?"

"Some of that punch would be good. I'm not in the mood for soda." He took a bite from a meatball and watched as Hal filled his cup. *This guy has a real servant's heart. Then again* — he looked around the room — *they all do.*

Gripping the plate in his left hand, Nathan took hold of the cup of punch with his right. He swallowed down a big drink. "That's good stuff."

"My wife made it," Hal confided, his voice a bit concealed. "I've had that same punch at over twenty parties this year alone." He laughed so loud, his joy reverberated around the room. "I can't stand the stuff, but she loves it." He gave Nathan a knowing wink, and his voice softened again. "These women of ours. They're good at what they do, aren't they? And their hearts are as big as Texas."

Nathan looked across the room at Kellie, who held Madison in her arms. "Uh, yes."

Hal dove off into a conversation about

goings-on at the church, and Nathan found himself squarely in the middle of a debate over whether or not the Prime Timers should replace their worn chairs with new ones. He didn't mind. In fact, he rather enjoyed the one-on-one time with Hal. Felt almost . . . natural.

At one point he shot another glance in Kellie's direction. Her face was alight with joy as she bounced Madison up and down on her hip.

That's a side of her I've never seen before. She looks . . . natural. Nearly everything about Kellie felt natural here. She fit in here. She was at home here. And there was a glow about her, something he couldn't quite place. Perhaps it was the pleasure of being in a place where so much love abounded.

His heart twisted with that revelation. Now that her father was doing better, perhaps he and Kellie could talk about going home again. He hoped she would carry some of this joy with her.

Kellie didn't know when she'd ever had a better night. As she looked around the now-messy room, her heart swelled with joy. In one night everything she had hoped and prayed for this past month had finally come to pass. Her father had returned home. Her sister had joined them. And Nathan was able to be here, relaxed and well rested. He'd visited with everyone in the room, from young to old. And she —

She felt a sense of anticipation, as if some private door to the world had opened up just for her. She couldn't figure out why. In years past she might have attributed this feeling to something going on at work, but this time things felt different. This time her wants and wishes had changed. *Substantially.*

Occasionally she would catch Nathan's gaze from across the room. He seemed more himself tonight — certainly more so than last Sunday morning. Something had happened that day — she suspected exhaustion had driven him to a point of frustration. But his countenance had improved by midday. And now, nearly a week later, he seemed a new man. *Reformed.*

She watched as he popped a cookie into his mouth, then chatted with Frankie at length. They were surely discussing his car — the latest gadgets and gizmos he hoped to add to it for better performance. Or perhaps they had slipped off into a conversation about the city's financial woes. She hoped not. Why ruin a perfectly good night?

On the other hand, she had hoped Nathan

would take an interest in the town's plight, hadn't she? With his brilliant mind at work, they might stand a chance at turning things around.

Kellie looked at the men with a more discerning eye. Frankie had a broad smile on his face.

"Having a good time?"

Kellie turned as she heard her mother's voice. "Mm-hmm. I'm so glad Daddy's home. I know you are, too."

Her mother's eyes filled with tears. "I am. I'm a little nervous, though. I hope I can take care of him."

"You'll have a nurse stopping by every day, right?"

Her mother sighed. "Yes. She'll be a big help. But he's taking so much medicine, and he'll have to be driven back and forth to physical therapy every day. It's a lot. I hope I'm up to it."

For the first time, Kellie noticed the extent of the weariness in her mother's eyes. She reached out and touched her arm. "I'll be here with you, Mom. I'm not going anywhere. You won't have to go through this by yourself, I promise."

Her mother nodded, and her short gray curls bobbed up and down. "I appreciate that, honey. I don't know how I could have made it through any of this without you. I've thanked God every day for sending you back. And I know your father has, too."

"I wouldn't have done anything differently." She embraced her mother, then gestured to Nathan. "And it looks as if he's starting to fit in."

"I've spent a lot of time praying about that." Her mother's brow wrinkled. "He's been so patient with all of us. But I'd imagine he'll be happy to get back home before long."

Home. For the first time in a while, Kellie thought about her life in Houston and cringed. *Lord, please don't send us back yet. Give me a few more weeks — a little more time here.*

She looked up as Julia's familiar laughter rang out across the room. Madison made a face as she bit into a large dill pickle. Everyone nearby watched her with broad smiles.

"That little girl is a doll," Kellie said.

"She is," her mother acknowledged. "And Julia is such a great mom."

Kellie grew silent and allowed her thoughts to roam as her mother moved on to talk to a friend. The desire for a child had come on Kellie gradually since arriving in Greenvine. What was it about this place

that made her think she could settle down
— give up everything she had worked and
planned for — and live a simple, uncompli-
cated life?

She found herself almost envying Julia and
Frankie. True, they didn't have much in the
way of material things, but they clearly
shared a love and faith in their future. In
some ways they seemed better prepared to
face the days ahead than she and Nathan
were, though they had given it their best effort.

Kellie continued to watch Madison from
a distance. She felt the familiar pangs of
desire but pressed them down. It didn't
make any sense to dream about such things.
Not yet anyway. Everything in God's time.

Oh, how she wished she knew more about
His time frame!

Kellie started as Nathan slipped his arm
around her waist.

"You're mighty quiet tonight."

"Am I?" She turned to face him with a
smile. "I don't mean to be. Just so happy."

"Me, too." He pressed kisses onto her
forehead, and she melted into his embrace
with a happy sigh.

"I love you, Nathan."

"I love you, too."

She pushed back the lump in her throat.

"I'm so grateful to you. I don't know how I can ever thank you for giving me this season with my dad."

"I'm so happy he's doing better. Maybe things will be back to normal before long."

Back to normal. Kellie gave him a weak smile. "Right now I'm happy to be with all the people I love."

"Me, too." He pressed another soft kiss on her brow. "You, especially."

She blushed a little but allowed him to give her a warm kiss in front of the whole room. Who cared if others knew they loved one another? She wasn't ashamed to show her affection for her husband. Not here, among friends and family.

After a moment alone, Kellie and Nathan made the rounds to say their good nights. Then, as the crowd thinned and her father retreated to the quiet of his bedroom, they made the drive home.

Once there, they enjoyed some quiet time together. Here, in this country place with no distractions, Kellie could think more clearly, give more freely, and even love more deeply.

With the taste of her husband's kisses still sweet on her lips, she eventually drifted off to sleep, content.

CHAPTER 15

Over the next two weeks, Kellie settled into a happy routine. She awoke each morning, had her quiet time with the Lord, spent a few hours on the Internet and the telephone, then went to her parents' home. Along the way, she enjoyed the flowers that bloomed in every yard and noticed the variety of trees. She waved to now-familiar neighbors and lowered the windows in the car so she could enjoy the fresh air.

Once she arrived at her parents' place, she helped her mother with everything from cleaning the kitchen to driving her father to physical therapy. Their hours were spent telling stories of days gone by, listening to music together, and discussing the prayer needs of friends at church. Occasionally they would go out to lunch at the cafeteria in Brenham and stop off at the outlet mall on the way home.

By the time she got back to the house,

Kellie had enough time to decide what to cook for dinner and tidy up a bit. Then, when Nathan arrived home, they talked about their day, ate together, and spent some time watching television or cuddling.

Occasionally they'd have dinner at Frankie and Julia's place. Kellie marveled at her friend's ability to balance everything — her workload at the school, her activities at the civic center, her daughter, and her marriage.

Or was it the other way around? As she watched, it became clear that Julia put her family well above her work. In fact, she spent more time talking about the people in her life than things.

Kellie took careful notes.

And she observed something else. In the past week, her friend's waistline had expanded a bit. Kellie watched in amazement. How wonderful and how frightening all at the same time. Julia's cheeks carried a rosy glow, and she beamed like a ray of sunshine when the ultrasound revealed the baby's sex: a boy. Their little family would be complete, at least for now.

Kellie couldn't imagine what it must feel like — or what she would look like if the same blessing were bestowed on her. She tried not to dwell on the pangs that gripped her heart each time she held a baby in her arms. Instead, she fought to ignore them. But a seed of hope had secretly begun to grow, one she'd have to share with Nathan soon or push to the back once and for all.

On Thursday afternoon, as she arrived back at the little wood-framed house, Kellie looked the place over with an inquisitive eye. In her somewhat overactive imagination, she could see it developing into a fine-looking home. Knock down a wall here; put up a wall there. Install new windows; replace the tub and tile. She could see it. And with the size of the property, they could expand when the time came.

She spent a moment reflecting. Something about this tiny place continued to captivate her. What was it? Perhaps it was the idea that a family had once lived here. Children had played in that yard — chasing one another and throwing balls. A wife and mother had cooked in the tiny dilapidated kitchen. A loving father had cradled his child in that living room.

Kellie thought about Mr. Henderson specifically now. She prayed for his health and his treatments. Soon she would see him again. But in the meantime, she wondered what his life had been like in earlier days as he resided in this very spot. Had he watched his children swing from the tire hanging in the front yard? Had he watched his daughters grow into young women, entering the front door with beaux on their arms? Had he cared for his ailing wife in the bedroom they had once shared? Had he watched the rooms grow empty as, one by one, his life became solitary?

A little shiver ran through Kellie, and she prayed for him again. How sad to live to such an old age and be alone. She thought about her own parents — how rich and full their lives were. What made the difference?

Relationships. Family. Friends. These things they all took for granted. And these were the very things she would sacrifice when she left Greenvine and moved back to Houston.

"Don't think like this," she scolded herself. "It's not going to make things easier. Pretty soon you'll be going back home."

Home.

She could scarcely remember what the condominium looked like. How could she ever feel at home there?

And yet she must prepare herself to return. Tonight, when Nathan arrived home, she would open the door to that conversation. She had put it off long enough. Now that her father's physical therapy sessions were dropping to twice a week, Kellie's list of excuses for staying in Greenvine had dwindled rapidly. She must come to terms with it.

But would the brokerage firm take her back full-time? She'd been assured it wouldn't be a problem, but situations weren't always what they presented themselves to be. Regardless, she must do her best to shift her thoughts in that direction. Already, Kellie had given the matter over to prayer. Now she must remove her hands from it altogether. Surely God was big enough to handle the pain this decision caused. Surely He could deal with her broken heart.

Nathan pulled his car out onto Highway 290 West in the direction of Greenvine. He'd fought traffic for the past thirty minutes, but things seemed to be thinning out now. It was the first moment all day he could relax and spend a little time thinking and planning. And with so much on his mind, preparing for the future came naturally.

Joy filled Nathan, coupled with a sense of anticipation. The Lord was surely at work in his life. All the pieces to his puzzle seemed to be coming together. Things at work were finally slowing down; he and

Kellie would soon be headed back home to Houston. And the best surprise of all — he had booked a trip to Europe for late summer. He could hardly wait to tell her. She would be thrilled.

Nathan let his mind dwell on the details for a moment. They would fly into Frankfurt and take that much-anticipated boat ride up the Rhine. They would tour ancient castles and find the perfect place to renew their wedding vows.

Just as Kellie had suggested months ago.

To cap things off they would drive into Austria and Switzerland to look at the mountains. Nathan practically beamed with excitement. Kellie would be so proud of him for taking matters into his own hands and planning this trip. Sure, it had put a damper on his savings plans for this summer, but who cared? Nathan felt like a man released from prison.

"Thank You, Lord — for freeing me from the idea that I have to store up treasures for myself. Kellie is my treasure. . . . *You* are my treasure."

These lessons had come from the past six weeks in Greenvine, to be sure. The Lord had been teaching, and Nathan had been on a learning curve. His well-laid plans for the future now paled in comparison to what he had in front of him at this very moment.

Kellie. Nathan smiled. The past few nights, in particular, she'd shown her love more than in years past. "Must be something in the water," he reasoned. Whatever it was, he hoped it lasted.

No. No complaints in that area. And he could find little to complain about in other areas either, now that he thought about it. Their life together seemed more simplistic, quieter, and more intimate. Even their conversations were better directed, more heartfelt.

And his sweet Kellie — always the last one to arrive at every function — seemed to be showing up every place on time these days. The frenzied look had left her eye. She was a well-rested version of her earlier self, and he liked what he saw.

Now, if only that bliss would follow them back to Houston, he would truly be a happy man.

Houston. Nathan thought about the city with a smile. Kellie would soon be back in the condominium, fussing over her latest purchase or complaining about the parking situation. She would buzz around the place, preparing for the workday ahead. She would settle back into the routine quickly. *I know her. She loves to work. She loves what she does.*

Moving back to Houston seemed logical. Still something bugged him, something he couldn't put his finger on. He tapped his finger on the steering wheel. *What is it, Lord? Why do I have this nagging thought something remains undone?*

Aha. There was still that one unanswered question about the financial trouble in Greenvine. But it wasn't his problem to solve. He didn't live in Greenvine. *Not really.* Of course it probably wouldn't hurt to make a few calls, check on a couple of things. And maybe, now that Kenton was home from the hospital, he might feel well enough to answer a few questions, offer some clarity.

These things often turned out to be a simple misunderstanding. Perhaps he could take a little time to help the fine people of Greenvine sort things out. After all, they had been mighty good to him.

Nathan reflected on his new friendships for the rest of the trip. He smiled as he thought about Hal pulling that catfish from the river. The loving older man had measured the monstrous fish, bragged about its size, then tossed it back into the water with a cockeyed grin. And that comment about the punch had thrown him for a loop. Who would've thought the fellow didn't care for his wife's prized punch recipe?

And Frankie — Nathan marveled at his new friend. Though worlds apart in so many ways, they shared a kindred spirit, of sorts. Nathan admired Frankie's work ethic — how he'd taken that little garage and turned it into a profitable shop. Still, in spite of his business, Frankie's world seemed fairly simplistic. In fact, he and Julia seemed to live the most carefree life Nathan had ever witnessed. A simple home, a precious little girl, and another child on the way.

Child on the way. There was something else he'd left undone. Nathan knew Kellie longed to talk about the possibility of children. Now that they were headed back home, he felt released to start thinking in that direction. *Perhaps in Europe.* He pondered the thought. What better idea than to conceive a child in some wonderful, foreign place? Yes, that trip would be the start of something new — in many ways.

As he pulled the car into the driveway, Nathan looked at the house. He had to smile, remembering what it had looked like that first day. Kellie had since painted the shutters and replaced the front door. Even the yard looked better, now that Jerry Chandler had invested some time and elbow grease. She had even talked the young man into putting in some new springtime flowers last Saturday.

Nathan rubbed at his chin, deep in thought. Yes, the home had surely made progress.

Then again, so had he.

CHAPTER 16

Kellie sighed as she looked around the cluttered kitchen. She stretched to grab something from the top cupboard but couldn't quite reach. "Nathan, can you come and help me with this?"

He entered the room, and she laughed at his appearance. His ragged T-shirt and faded jeans looked a little out of place on him. And the tennis shoes, once white, were now covered in splotches of paint. He even had paint in his hair.

"Wow. That's quite a fashion statement." She giggled.

He shrugged. "No point in getting dressed up just to work on the house. I want to get that back bedroom finished before Mr. Henderson gets here."

Kellie drew in a sigh. Yes, Chuck Henderson was due to arrive in a couple of hours. She wondered how he would take the news that they were moving out of the house earlier than planned. Perhaps he missed the place and was ready to return home. That would make things easier.

Then again — she looked around with a smile. This was hardly the same home he'd left behind two months ago. The space had been transformed. *Literally.* Would he feel like a stranger in his own house?

Nathan interrupted her thoughts. "Did you need me for something?"

"Oh." She started to attention. "Yes. I'm trying to get those plastic storage containers." She pointed to the top cupboard. "But I can't reach."

"Not a problem." He pulled the containers down, one by one. "What do you want me to do with them?"

She sighed again. "I guess just leave them on the counter for now. I'm almost out of boxes." She looked around the kitchen at the five large boxes she'd already taped up. "Which reminds me — would you mind carrying these out to the garage?"

"Sure." Nathan reached to pick up one. "But remember — you don't have to get all of this done today. We don't have to be home for another week or so. And we could always come back and get the rest later."

"I know. But my weekdays are already taken up with work and several last-minute things for my parents." She brushed aside the mist of tears that mounted her lashes. "And I want to spend every minute I can with them while we're still here."

"I understand." Nathan gave her a gentle peck on the cheek. "But Rome wasn't built in a day, and you sure don't have to get everything packed up right away."

He looked around the kitchen, lips pursed. "What are we going to do with all this stuff back in Houston anyway?"

"I'll leave a lot of it here," she explained. "I'm sure Mr. Henderson would like to have it. It's certainly newer — nicer — than what he had."

"True." Nathan headed out to the garage, and Kellie threw herself back into her work. After a few minutes, however, she had to take a break. For some reason the day's activities had worn her out.

Nathan finished with the rest of the boxes, then plopped down onto the sofa next to her. "Ready for some lunch? I'm starving."

"Mmm." Her stomach growled, but the idea of food didn't sound terribly appealing. Not yet anyway. "I guess. What did you have in mind?"

"Let's see what we have in here." He stepped into the kitchen, opened the refrigerator, and pulled out all sorts of things.

"Turkey. Ham. Lettuce. Mayo. Two kinds of cheese — Monterey Jack and Swiss. And we still have plenty of that homemade oat bread Julia sent over."

"Mmm."

He stood in the doorway. "Want me to make a couple of sandwiches? You look beat."

"I am." She leaned back against the sofa. "I guess you were right. I've been trying to do too much too fast."

"Told you. But rest for now. I'm on it." He returned to the kitchen, and she could hear him slapping sandwiches together.

A few minutes later, he entered the living room with two plates in hand. "Sandwiches, chips, and a soda for my lady." He extended a plate in her direction, and she took it willingly.

"Thanks. I think I am hungry. Starving, actually." She took the plate and set it on the coffee table, smiling as she noticed he'd garnished the sandwich with a pickle.

"It's my cooking," he bragged. "You can't turn it down."

Kellie wasn't sure when she'd ever seen him look so proud. Or so adorable.

"Right, right." She smiled and bit into the sandwich. "Mmm. Not bad."

"Not bad?" His lips curled down. "Come

190

on and admit it. That's the best sandwich you've ever eaten."

She put on her most serious face. "It's okay."

"Okay?"

Kellie chuckled. "It's mahvelous, dahling. Simply mahvelous!"

A look of relief swept across Nathan's face. "That's more like it."

They chatted as they ate. Kellie tried to force a smile as he talked about their plans for the future, especially the part about going to Europe.

Funny, though. Right now even Europe doesn't sound that appealing. Lord, help me get beyond what I'm thinking and feeling. I need to be with my husband — not just physically, but psychologically and emotionally.

They talked of Europe and other things as they finished their lunch. Afterward Kellie returned to her work in the kitchen. She smiled as she looked at the new appliances. Mr. Henderson would be tickled pink at the changes. She only hoped he didn't mind the house sitting empty until he could return. She and Nathan would continue to pay rent until the agreed time anyway.

At two thirty a knock on the door interrupted her work. She pulled the door open to find a much thinner Chuck Henderson standing on the other side. He still maintained the same mischievous eyes. A young woman stood next to him, her arm linked through his.

"Mr. Henderson." Kellie extended her hand. "Welcome home."

"Thank you."

He gave her hand a light shake, and she noticed he was clearly weaker than the last time she'd seen him.

"How have you been?" She asked the question tentatively.

He flashed a cockeyed grin, and a glimpse of his former personality emerged. "Fitter'n a fiddle." He turned his attention to the nice-looking young woman who stood at his side. "This is my daughter, Linda."

Kellie extended her hand toward the young woman, who looked to be not much older than she was. "It's so nice to meet you. Thanks for coming out on such short notice. Please have a seat." She gestured toward the sofa.

Linda nodded. "Look what they've done with the place, Daddy," she said with an admiring smile. "It's beautiful. It hardly looks like the little house I grew up in." She smiled as she looked at Kellie. "Not that that's a bad thing. It looks great."

"Thank you. I'll get my husband, and

we'll be right with you." Kellie headed down the hallway to fetch Nathan.

As he entered the living room, Nathan extended his hand. "Good to see you again, Mr. Henderson."

"None of this Mr. Henderson stuff," the older man said with the wave of his hand. "Call me Chuck."

"Chuck." Nathan nodded and sat on the couch next to Kellie. She gestured for Chuck and his daughter to sit across from them.

"Nice to see you, too. I . . ." Chuck hesitated and looked at his daughter, who gave him a reassuring nod. "I've been meaning to get by to talk to the two of you anyway."

Ah. He's wanting to come home sooner than expected. That will make things so much easier.

"You have?" Nathan asked.

Mr. Henderson looked down at his hands. "I have. And now that I'm here, I feel more confident than ever." He gazed around the room. "You have done wonders with the place, just like Linda said."

"Thank you." Kellie and Nathan spoke in unison.

"Not exactly my taste," the older man acknowledged, "but still it's nice."

Kellie felt her cheeks flush. "Well, we can always recarpet if you like."

"No, no." His eyebrows furrowed a bit. "Don't want you to do that. You've gone to a lot of trouble already."

"Well, it's your home. We want you to —"

"It's like this," Mr. Henderson interrupted. "I've decided not to come back."

"What?" Nathan's face paled, and Kellie was afraid for a moment he might overreact.

An embarrassed grin crossed the older man's face. "I never thought I'd live to see the day, but it turns out I like big-city life."

His daughter smiled. "As if anyone could call Brenham a big city." She rested her hand across her father's arm. "But, to be honest, we love having Daddy with us. Our boys adore him, and our house is so big. We have plenty of room."

"They've got cable television." Mr. Henderson grinned. "Two hundred channels." He nodded matter-of-factly, as if that settled the deal.

"So" — Kellie glanced at Nathan for help — "so what were you thinking? You're going to sell the house?"

"That's right." The older man's gaze shifted down to his hands. "Look — I know it's not worth much. It's not big-city living, for sure. But it's very homey, and it sure

looks like you two have taken a liking to it."
He gestured with his hand. "You've pert
near turned it into a palace. And besides"
— he looked at his daughter again — "I
could sure use the money. Medicare covers
most of my treatments, but I don't have any
real insurance to speak of."

Kellie felt a lump in her throat. How could
they tell him they planned to move out next
week? "Oh, Mr. Henderson."

"Daddy tends to worry too much." Linda
patted her father's hand. "I don't think
there's much to be concerned about financially, but it would ease his mind a great
deal if he could sell the house. That would
be one less thing for him to think about."

Nathan cleared his throat and looked in
Kellie's direction. She wondered how he
would handle this, what he would say. His
cheeks flushed red, a sure sign thoughts
were stirring. But what sort of thoughts?

"Would you excuse us a moment?" Nathan asked.

He took Kellie by the hand, and they
made their way down the hall toward the
master bedroom. They entered and sat on
the bed. Neither of them said a word.
Finally Kellie broke the silence.

"Oh, Nathan." She buried her face in her
hands. "What are we going to do?" She

lifted her face to gaze into his eyes.

He drew in a deep breath, forehead wrinkled. "Well, I have an idea. I don't know how you'll feel about it, but here goes."

As he laid out his plan, Kellie's mind eased at once. It was the only thing that made sense. Yes, it would require great sacrifice on their part, to be sure, but they had grown accustomed to sacrifice over the past several months.

Yes, she reasoned. *This could work.*

With her husband's hand tightly clutched in her own, Kellie traipsed back up the hallway to give Mr. Henderson the news.

Nathan returned to Houston on Monday morning, his head full of ideas. He stopped by the condo on his way into the office to check the mail. He smiled as he looked around the place. *Quite a contrast to our current living conditions.* He and Kellie had nearly grown used to living with middle-of-the-road furnishings and appliances. But not for long.

Their time in Greenvine was rapidly drawing to a close. Boxes were packed and cupboards nearly bare. Soon — in less than a week — they would be here again. Where they belonged. It would require at least one truckload of boxes, but they'd see to that

196

this coming Saturday. Once they got settled in, he and Kellie would travel back and forth to Greenvine on the weekends as they had planned from the beginning.

Not that he'd minded the past few weeks. Truth be told, Nathan had grown to love the people of Greenvine. And the changes he and Kellie had faced over the past seven weeks had made him a better man.

Nathan drew in a satisfied breath and thought about how he'd drawn closer to God during this season. And the Lord responded by speaking, giving direction. Nathan heard His voice clearly these days, with much more clarity than in years past.

His decision regarding the house in Greenvine had been God-inspired, to be sure. They would buy the property from Mr. Henderson and rent it out. With a little TLC, the home would make for a great investment.

Of course he must take care of the technicalities. A Realtor would have to be hired, and the repairs would need to take place right away for the house to pass inspection. But Nathan didn't mind, especially since he wouldn't be the one doing the work. He couldn't — not with so much going on already.

"Nothing like taking a little more on your

plate when it's already full." Nathan smiled. "But we're getting pretty good at balancing a lot at once."

He pulled his car into the parking garage at the accounting firm and shut it down. For a moment he leaned his head back against the headrest and prayed. All the pieces to his puzzle seemed to be coming together. *Well, almost all.*

Why couldn't he get Greenvine's financial problems off his mind?

He knew why. After several phone calls last Friday, the truth was clear. The city had been taken for a ride and had lost a small fortune — almost enough to sink them if someone didn't intervene — and quickly.

Nathan's concern for his father-in-law deepened with each revelation. Kenton had been taken advantage of, to be sure. He had acted out of honesty and sincerity and clearly felt awful about the whole thing. No one held him to blame. That's how the people of Greenvine were. They cared far too much about him to point any fingers. And right now his health required that he remain positive, upbeat.

Nathan sighed as he contemplated the most worrisome thing. His father-in-law's ability to reason clearly had not returned — at least not in full. Perhaps in time. But for now he couldn't handle the situation. He could barely handle the small things, like dressing himself and fixing a bowl of cereal each morning. How could he be called upon to save the city from financial ruin?

Lord, I don't understand. It's too much for one man to handle.

"He needs help solving this." Nathan pursed his lips. "But what can I do? It's too late to recoup their money."

The best chance the city of Greenvine stood right now was a concise, practical investment plan for the future. They'd probably need to raise taxes a little to accomplish this and would need someone they could trust to advise them regarding future investments. Someone with a head for financial matters. And someone who genuinely cared about the townspeople — cared about more than their financial interests. Someone who cared about them as people, not as taxpayers.

Nathan's thoughts flashed back to the night he'd been honored as Man of the Year. What was it Mr. Abernathy had said of him? *"Please welcome Nathan Fisher — a man with a head for numbers and a heart for the people. He's one of the hardest workers I've ever meet, and he's our Man of the Year at Siefert and Collins."*

Nathan trembled as the words rolled through his memory. "Oh, Lord, surely You're not asking me to do this thing." *Surely not.*

He reached for his briefcase and sprinted from his car, forcing the ludicrous idea from his mind.

CHAPTER 17

Kellie paced around the house with a string of nonsensical prayers flowing. *Lord, I don't understand. What are You up to? Oh, Lord, I'm going to need Your help.*

This changes everything.

She stared down at the white plastic stick in her hand for the umpteenth time. *Yep. Positive.* Just like the last million times she'd looked at it.

"Pregnant." She spoke to the empty room. But how? They had been so careful. If truth stared her in the face, then the Lord certainly had a sense of humor.

And interesting timing. Kellie plopped down onto the sofa, deep in thought. How in the world could she accomplish working full-time and raising a baby? And where would she raise it? They had no room in their tiny condo for a child. One bedroom. One medium-sized, not-ready-for-anyone-else bedroom.

And Nathan. What would he think? Would he assume she had planned this to trap him?

"Oh, Lord. You've got to help me. I don't know how to tell him."

Then again she couldn't go without telling him for long. Her body had begun to betray her. What had started out as mere queasiness a week ago had developed into full-blown sessions of toilet-hugging. Every morning for the past three days, she'd spent more time in the bathroom than out. She was thankful Nathan had already left for work before the episodes began.

Clueless. He's clueless.

The phone rang, and Kellie nearly jumped out of her skin. She glanced at the caller ID. *Nathan.*

She tried to sound as normal as possible as she answered. "Hello?"

"Hey, babe," his cheery voice greeted her. "I just got to the office. Thought I'd call and check on you."

"Oh?"

"You were sleeping like a rock when I left." He sniggered. "I haven't heard snoring like that in a while."

She groaned. *I'm snoring for two now.* "I'm fine. I'm about to start packing up the bedroom. And I have a couple of calls to make. Bernie wants me to come in Monday

202

morning. I hope I'm up to it by then. This weekend is going to be crazy." *Maybe crazier than we thought.*

"I know. That's part of the reason I'm calling. I rented a small moving truck. I'll pick it up in Brenham on Friday night. I don't think we'll need anything more than that. And Frankie said he'll come by Saturday morning to help load up. That means I only have to find someone to help once we get back to the condo."

"Right. Well, I appreciate him, for sure." *I can't do any heavy lifting now.*

Kellie listened as Nathan carried on about how they would transport the two cars back and forth but didn't take much in. Instead, her mind wandered to the obvious. She put her hand on her stomach and waited for something to happen.

Nothing.

"Kellie? You there?"

She jolted back to reality as she heard Nathan's voice. "Oh yeah. I'm sorry. I'm distracted today. Too much on my mind."

"That will end soon." His voice resonated with calm, practical assurance. "Before you know it, we'll be back home and everything will be back to normal."

"Yeah." She glanced down at the white stick. *Still positive.* "Back to normal."

"Well, almost normal anyway." He paused for a moment, and she felt a shift in the conversation. "Things at work are — strange. That's the only way I can describe it. Everything is so hush-hush around here today. I don't know what's up, but I get the feeling something's about to blow."

"Yikes. No clues?"

"No," he said. "But I'm trying not to read too much into it. In fact, I've been a little distracted myself. To be honest, there's something I can't stop thinking about. Something completely unrelated to the firm."

As he paused, Kellie felt the queasiness return. She drew in a deep breath and waited for it to pass. "W–what do you mean?"

"I, uh, I was trying to figure out how to go about offering my help to your dad. I can't get Greenvine's financial issues off my mind."

"Ah. I see." She ignored the tingling in her cheeks as she contemplated his words. Had the Lord convinced him of this? Were they supposed to be getting involved? "I've spent a lot of time praying and thinking about it myself," Kellie acknowledged. "And I think we could help them. But it would take time. Effort."

"Right." He sighed. "That's the hard part. I don't have a lot of time right now. And my efforts seem to be so divided already." He sighed. "And once we get back home . . ." His voice trailed off. "I don't know, Kell. It just seems impossible. But if it's impossible, then why won't the Lord leave me alone? Why does He keep dropping this into my heart, into my spirit?"

Fresh feelings of nausea rose and then settled down almost as quickly. Kellie was better able to focus on the conversation, to take in the full meaning of his words. "I can't answer that, babe," she said. "But if God is speaking, all I can say is, we'd better be listening."

A dead silence permeated the air for a moment. When Nathan finally responded, his words startled her. "I don't think I like what I'm hearing. Is that awful?"

Kellie forced back a smile. If he thought his news complicated things, wait until he heard what she had to say.

Another call interrupted them, and Nathan had to leave abruptly. With the telephone still in her hand, Kellie looked heavenward. "Lord, I'm not sure what You're up to." She glanced at the house full of boxes. "But I hope You'll show me before I pack another thing."

Nathan pulled his car into the condo's parking garage. *Great.* Someone had taken his spot. Again. With frustration mounting, he drove up to the top floor and parked on the roof. He needed time to think anyway.

He shut off the car and grabbed his laptop. With a determined stride, he headed for the elevator. On the way there, his thoughts jumped from one thing to another. *The office.* He contemplated today's revelations. Things at Siefert and Collins were definitely in a state of transition. Today, less than an hour ago, he'd been offered a new position at the firm.

Partner.

Finally Nathan had been offered the coveted position he'd prayed for.

"Why don't I feel right about this? What's wrong with me? I should be calling Kellie. I should be celebrating."

A *ding* brought him back to his senses. He stepped into the elevator and punched the number seven. Surely a good night's sleep would put everything in perspective. He leaned back against the elevator wall and closed his eyes.

By the time the elevator arrived at his

floor, Nathan resolved himself to the inevitable. He must pick up the phone and let Kellie know, even if she recognized the discomfort in his voice. He must keep this ball rolling. It was too late to stop it now.

He trudged along the hallway until he reached his condominium. The maintenance man greeted him outside the door.

"Good evening, Mr. Fisher."

Nathan eyed him suspiciously. "Bobby. Is everything okay?"

"Well . . ."

"It's okay. Just tell me, whatever it is."

Bobby tucked a flashlight into his tool bag. "The AC unit froze up this morning. We've had to shut everything down in order to thaw it out. We'll probably have everything up and running by tomorrow."

"Right. Tomorrow."

Nathan pulled at his collar as he braved the heat inside the condo. He checked the thermostat. Eighty-two degrees. "It's not even summer yet. Why is it so ridiculously hot?"

Nathan pulled off his shirt and slacks and slipped into a T-shirt and shorts. Then he scrounged around in the kitchen, looking for something to eat. They would have to do some heavy-duty grocery shopping once they moved back for good. For now he decided on a can of soup and some stale crackers.

He settled onto the sofa with a bowl in hand. As he ate, Nathan reached for the remote control. He listened to the evening news in shocked silence. Were the stories always this negative, or was his hometown just suffering a particularly bad day?

He switched the channel, choosing an old movie. Not five minutes into it, he muted the television and picked up the telephone to call Kellie. He needed to hear her voice and needed to tell her about his promotion. She would cheer him up. She would bring everything into balance.

Kellie answered with an unusually weary sound to her voice. She went on to assure him everything was fine, but the conversation left Nathan feeling uneasy. As he told her about the partnership, he expected to hear rejoicing on the other end of the phone. For some reason her voice seemed to choke up.

She's just happy for me.

She ended the call rather abruptly — something about needing to turn off the bathwater. Nathan tried to take it in stride but felt in his spirit something was wrong.

He dropped into bed a little before nine, exhausted and frustrated. His thoughts shifted for hours between the job, the sale of the house, and Greenvine's financial problems. Sleeping was out of the question, especially with the heat presenting such an issue.

At two fifteen he arose from the bed and walked out onto the balcony. He stood in silence for a moment as he rubbed at his aching brow. The hum of traffic from the street below provided the perfect backdrop. Nathan sank into the deck chair and leaned back with his eyes closed. He couldn't possibly make it through this night without focusing.

Not on himself or his problems, but on the Lord.

CHAPTER 18

Nathan picked up a small moving van in Brenham on Friday night. With Kellie following along behind him in her car, he traveled the now-familiar road toward Greenvine. On the way there, his thoughts tumbled round in his head. He contemplated not the move but the meeting he'd just called at the civic center.

He glanced at his watch. 6:48. In twelve minutes city leaders, his father-in-law included, would converge upon the tiny civic center for an informative gathering Nathan had initiated after a near-sleepless night. Once there, he would lay out the financial plan that hadn't given him a moment's rest.

A plan to save the city of Greenvine.

Nathan turned off onto the country road that led to the center of town. The moving van jolted up and down with each pothole. His nerves, once jumbled and on edge, settled down, in spite of the bumpy road. Now that a plan had formed, his body seemed more relaxed.

He glanced in the side mirror to catch a glimpse of Kellie's vehicle. Her sports car seemed tiny in comparison to this monstrous van. But still she looked regal, sitting behind the wheel.

He loved to see her like that, in a seat of honor. She deserved it. No one worked harder than Kellie or had loftier plans. She was truly a queen — and not just the queen of quick, as she called herself. She sat like royalty upon his heart.

He squinted against the setting sun to see her face more clearly. Immediately concern registered. Were those tears? He rolled down the window and twisted the mirror a bit, trying to get a better look. Why would she be crying?

His heart twisted as the truth prevailed. She was sad about leaving Greenvine. He knew that. He'd always known this transition back to Houston would be tough on her, but — *tears?* Kellie wasn't a crier, by any stretch.

He looked in the mirror again — and nearly drove the vehicle off the road in the process. "Stay focused, man." He gripped the steering wheel, unable to remember where he was headed. Kellie's emotions now consumed his thoughts.

She was clearly keeping her tears hidden from him. She was going along with his plans and not saying a word. *But why?* Was she scared to tell him how she felt?

Nathan drew in a deep breath as he turned down the road toward the civic center. As he bounced up and down in the cab of the moving van, reality hit. He'd made so many decisions, but had he somehow pressed the voice of the Lord to the background and shifted onto a road of his own? Had he left Kellie out? His thoughts drifted back to that day when he'd accused her of the same thing. She'd left him out of the equation initially, but who was to blame now?

He looked in the mirror again and caught a glimpse of Kellie drying her eyes with rushed fingertips. *She doesn't want me to know she's unhappy.*

His words with the Almighty now flowed from a place of truth — of open honesty.

"Lord, show me Your will. I've made so many plans. Have I asked You to come on board after the fact? If Your plans are different from mine —"

His heart quickened. If the Lord's plans were different, could he live with that?

Common sense kicked in. Of course the Lord wanted them in the city. He'd given them a clear-cut plan for their future.

Future.

The word hit hard as he glanced in the mirror once again. The future was — tomorrow. It wasn't the here and now. And what good was a happy tomorrow if you had a miserable today?

The revelation slammed against his seared conscience. He'd been living for the future and spending far too much time worrying about the outcome of life's situations.

The Lord, it turned out, was apparently more interested in the journey.

Kellie took a seat near the front of the room. She reached over to grip her daddy's hand and gave it a tight squeeze. "How are you feeling?" she whispered.

"Better." He gave her a wink, and her heart almost sang.

Almost. Another thought immediately put a damper on things. *We're leaving. Tomorrow. This is my last night with my family, for a while anyway.*

Kellie sat with her father's hand in her own as Nathan stood before the people. The crowd grew quiet as he began to speak. She listened with great joy as he outlined a detailed plan to get the city back on its feet. She wondered, though, how the citizens of Greenvine would take the news that they must begin again.

Begin again.

Hmm. She tried to still her trembling hands by placing them across her belly. Inside, life was beginning. A piece of her. A piece of Nathan. She would tell him soon. This news couldn't wait much longer.

As Nathan wrapped up his speech, the place came alive. One by one, the good folks of Greenvine poured out their questions, sought his counsel. He responded to each one thoughtfully and clearly with their best interests in mind. Kellie's heart swelled with pride as he took the time to think through his answers and voice them in love.

"That's quite a guy you've got there." Her father whispered the words into her ear, and she nodded with a lump in her throat.

"I know."

As the meeting drew to a close, Kellie joined the other women in the kitchen, preparing snacks for the crowd. They set out platters of fresh-cut vegetables and tempting fruit, and she entered into conversation with several of the ladies as they worked alongside one another.

"Nathan is so great," Julia observed. "I

mean" — she looked at him admiringly — "I've always known he was a great accountant. I guess I didn't realize he was so good at the people part. He's a good communicator, and he seems to care about us."

"He does." Kellie nodded. "I know because he's lost a lot of sleep over this." She didn't add that he'd called her three times in the night to ask her opinion on his ideas, particularly those related to investments. He cared about her expertise, as well, and had wanted to get her take on his plan. And she was happy to link arms with him on this project. In fact, she didn't know when she'd ever felt so good about anything.

Julia shrugged. "I guess it's pretty rare to find someone with a head for numbers and —"

Kellie finished for her with words that seemed to leap from her throat. "A heart for the people."

Why does that sound so familiar? Ah yes. They were Mr. Abernathy's words as he'd introduced Nathan a few short months ago.

She looked across the room at Nathan, who spoke with his hands to a group of men. They hung on his every word, nodding and patting him on the back. Nathan was brilliant, to be sure. But his love for people far exceeded any academic gifting.

Now, with the people behind him, he seemed to spring from his shell, energized by their enthusiasm.

Kellie turned back to her mother and Julia to wrap up her thoughts on the matter. "He wants to do what he can to make things better for you guys."

Her mother leaned over to give her a peck on the cheek. "He let you spend these last few weeks with us," she whispered. "That's definitely made things better for all of us. I don't know what I would've done without you."

Kellie reached up to give her mother a warm hug. "I'm going to miss you. But I need to be with Nathan, and he wants to be" — her voice broke — "back in Houston." She brushed at damp eyelashes.

"We wouldn't have it any other way, hon. You need to be together."

Kellie looked to the front of the room, where Nathan and her father stood in concentrated dialogue. The spark in her husband's eye intrigued her. She hadn't seen this kind of enthusiasm in him for a long time. In fact, she wasn't sure she'd ever seen him this excited, hopeful. She liked the new Nathan — and hoped it translated over into their new life in Houston.

New life.

How could she possibly begin a new life when she still harbored old feelings? *Lord, if You're wanting to renew my heart, to clean out the fear and anxiety, then do it. Have Your way, Father. I want to be in the center of Your will — no place else. And if that means Houston — then I'm fine with that.*

Kellie settled the issue once and for all in her heart. She would, as the scripture so aptly said, learn to be content in whatever state she found herself — genuinely, peacefully content.

She crossed the room to where Nathan now stood alone. She slipped her arm in his and gave him an adoring gaze.

He glanced down with a look of concern. "Are you okay?"

"Sure." She smiled up at him. "Why?"

"Oh, nothing." He brushed a stray hair out of her eye. "I just want you to be happy."

Kellie's heart twisted. "I — I am happy, honey."

"Really?" His brow furrowed, and she wondered if he'd been listening to her earlier thoughts.

Kellie's gaze shifted to the ground, and she fought back the tears. "I–I've loved every minute of being here," she said finally. "But I know we have to be where God wants us to be. And wherever that is, I'm okay."

He nodded but said nothing.

"I figure," Kellie continued with enthusiasm mounting, "that as long as we're in the center of God's will, we're in the safest place on earth, regardless of where we live. Right?"

He nodded again but said nothing.

"Where we are physically isn't half as important as where we are with Him." Kellie beamed now. "So wherever He calls us to go — I'm going. As long as you're going, too."

Nathan drew in a deep breath and pulled her close. He planted kisses in her hair and then whispered, "You're the smartest woman I know."

Kellie giggled. "Then you don't know many women — that's all I've got to say."

CHAPTER 19

Nathan awoke early on Saturday morning. He lay silent in the bed for a while, listening to Kellie breathe. For some time, he drank in the stillness of the moment.

Nothing could have prepared him for her sudden bolt from the bed. He watched in amazement as she sprinted toward the bathroom, hand over her mouth.

"What's wrong?" He followed her to the bathroom door, but she closed it in his face.

Kellie never answered, but he could hear the noise from the other side.

"You're sick?"

Still no answer. When she finally emerged from the room, her face was pale and drawn.

"Kellie?" He followed her to the bathroom sink, where she reached for a toothbrush.

She checked her appearance in the mirror. "Ugh. I look as bad as I feel." She slathered toothpaste on the brush and stuck it in her mouth.

"I'm sorry you're sick." Nathan reached to pull her hair out of her eyes as she brushed her teeth. "Do you think it's something you ate?"

She shook her head but never looked up.

"Some kind of stomach bug?"

She didn't answer. Instead, she continued to brush her teeth in silence. When she finished, she finally looked him in the eye. "I feel a lot better now. I'm sure I'll be fine."

"Still." He ran his hand along her cheek. "I want you to take it easy today. We've got lots of people coming to help. No need in you doing too much."

"I'll take it easy," she assured him. "But don't worry. I'm sure I'll be fine."

He nodded, then headed off to the shower. As the hot water beat down on his neck, Nathan planned for the day ahead. Frankie would arrive at nine. With his help they would load up the boxes and clothes. After that he and Kellie would hit the road for home. They would return to Greenvine next weekend to tie up loose ends and prepare the house for inspection.

Nathan exited the shower, his mind in a whirl. He tried not to let his thoughts slow down much. If they did . . .

No, he wouldn't stop to think. He must plow forward with the task at hand. He would have plenty of time to think later.

Once dressed, Nathan entered the bedroom. Surprise filled him as he looked at the bed where Kellie lay curled up, still in her nightgown.

"Not feeling any better?" he asked.

She sat up with a start. "Oh." She gave him a quizzical look. "I'm just —"

"It's okay, honey." He walked over and kissed her lightly. "I told you to take it easy."

He sat on the edge of the bed and ran his fingers through her hair. She pushed his hand away and rolled over.

"Are you mad at me?" Nathan asked.

She shook her head.

He wasn't convinced. "Do you want to talk about it?"

No response.

Nathan stood up and walked to his chest of drawers to pull out jeans and a T-shirt. How could he go about reading her mind? On the other hand, maybe she didn't want him to. Maybe she needed space.

He dressed quickly and headed to the kitchen to make some coffee. Moments later he sat at the table with a cup in his hand. A knock on the door roused him from his quiet thoughts. Nathan glanced at his watch. *8:42. Frankie's early.*

He trudged to the door and opened it,

startled to find his in-laws on the other side.

"Well, good morning." He greeted them with a hug.

"Can we come in?" Kenton asked.

"Of course." Nathan ushered them into the kitchen and offered them a cup of coffee.

They sat together at the table, and he quickly explained Kellie's absence.

"Should I go and check on her?" Norah asked.

He nodded, and his mother-in-law slipped off into the other room.

Kenton sat in silence for a moment, then finally looked Nathan in the eye. "Norah was doing me a favor by leaving," he explained with a twinkle in his eye. "She knows I came to speak with you. Guess she thought I needed some privacy."

"Privacy? What's up?" Nathan took a sip of coffee, then leaned back in his chair.

Kenton looked at him intently. "Nathan, I've got a problem."

Nathan laid a hand on his father-in-law's arm. "What do you mean?"

"I mean" — Kenton's gaze shifted down — "I'm not getting any younger. And even though I'm getting around better, I'm still — still —" He paused, and his eyes filled with tears. "This is what I'm trying to say,

Nathan. I don't believe I can return to my job. I've overstayed my welcome as it is."

"Sir?"

"The fine people of Greenvine have entrusted me with the position of city comptroller for years." Kenton spoke slowly, carefully. "But I'd be looking at retirement in another year or two anyway." He looked up, his eyes brimming over.

Nathan tried to swallow the growing lump in his throat. "What are you saying, Kenton?"

"I'm saying" — the older man stared directly into his eyes — "that I'm beyond the point where I can do this city any good. But you're not."

"Excuse me?"

"Nathan, you're a wonderful young man. You've been the answer to my daughter's prayers — and, in so many ways, an answer to our prayers. We never had the privilege of having a son, but the Lord has sent a fine one our way."

"Th–thank you, sir."

"God has blessed us in so many ways of late; I don't have any business asking for more." Kenton sighed. "But I feel it would be wrong of me not to mention what's been on my heart for the past several days, especially after the people took so well to your plan last night." He looked up, determination in his eyes. "I'll cut to the chase and save you any questions. Elections are just around the corner, and I think you'd make a fine city comptroller for the people of Greenvine."

Nathan set down the coffee cup with a thud. Surely the older man jested. City comptroller? To stay would require putting an end to everything he and Kellie had hoped and prayed for.

"I–I'm not sure what to say." He didn't dare look his father-in-law in the eye, not when his eyes would give away his feelings.

Kenton patted him on the back. "No need to say anything — at least not yet. Just promise me you'll pray about it."

Nathan nodded in numbed silence. *Pray about it?* A knock on the door brought him back to his senses. He glanced at his watch. 9:02. "That's Frankie."

"I'll get myself another cup of coffee." Kenton stood and headed toward the coffeemaker while Nathan plodded to the front door.

"Mornin', neighbor!" Frankie greeted him with a broad smile.

Nathan extended his hand. "Good morning to you, too. Thanks for coming to help."

"No problem." Frankie looked back toward the car. "I've enlisted the troops. Hope it's okay that we brought Madison along." He gestured toward Julia, who lifted Madison from the car seat.

"Of course." Nathan watched with a grin as the little girl squirmed in her mother's arms. Within seconds they joined him at the door.

"Where's Kellie?" Julia asked.

"In the bedroom with her mom." Nathan shrugged. "She's sick."

"No way." Julia trudged off in the direction of the bedroom, and Frankie and Nathan joined Kenton in the kitchen for a cup of coffee. They chatted about the weather, the construction on Highway 290 — everything but the move. Finally, when he could sit still no longer, Nathan stood. The time had come.

They'd better get packing.

Kellie spent a few minutes chatting with her mother and Julia before they stepped into the kitchen for a cup of coffee. She slipped out of her nightgown and robe and into some clothes before heading out to join them. She still battled queasiness but did her best to force it aside. No point in raising suspicions. Not yet anyway. She padded into the kitchen, which was filled with boxes.

"Where are the guys?" She tried to act casual as she reached for a coffee cup from the windowsill.

Her mother gestured out the front window. "They've already started loading up."

"Ah." She looked out of the window in time to see Nathan hoisting a box into the back of the moving truck. Her heart twisted a bit, but she pushed the feelings down.

"I should finish packing up these last few dishes." She opened a cupboard and pointed to a handful of things she'd deliberately held back till now.

"Let me help." Her mother stood right away. "I'm so sorry you're not feeling well this morning."

Kellie shrugged, hoping to still her mother's fears. "I'll be fine." She smiled warmly and changed the subject by turning to face Julia. "So when are you and Frankie coming to town to see us?"

"When do you want us?"

"As soon as you can get there." Kellie reached to grab her friend's hand and fought to keep the tears from rising.

"I'm not much of a city girl," Julia said with a shrug. "But for you, I'll give it a try."

They dove back into their work, chatting like schoolgirls. An hour or so later, a handful of people from the church showed up with food in their hands. They set up card tables on the lawn, then stayed to join in the fun. Shortly thereafter, others arrived with everything from sodas to homemade cookies. They added their food to the existing bounty, and the tiny tables overflowed.

By the time the guys had the truck loaded, lunchtime had arrived. Kellie joined the others on the lawn as they shared sandwiches, conversation, and laughter. It seemed no time at all had passed when Kellie looked at her watch and gasped. 1:25. They had planned to leave before noon.

She left the roar of the crowd for a moment to take one final look at the house. She didn't realize Nathan had joined her until she felt his arms slip around her waist from behind.

"We'll be back next weekend to finish up." He spoke quietly, but she detected an edge to his voice, something she couldn't define.

She nodded and turned to face him. "I know." She leaned her head against his shoulder and tried to relax.

"Kellie?"

She looked into his eyes. For some reason they were etched with concern.

"What, babe?"

He sighed deeply. "There's something I need to tell you before we go."

"Really?" She drew in a sigh of her own. "Because there's something I need to tell you, too."

CHAPTER 20

All morning long, Nathan had argued with himself, but the truth now raised its head, and he could not press it down any longer. What would be the point, when the voice of the Lord roared so loudly in his ears? Nathan plunged into the conversation with Kellie, spilling everything at once.

He told her about the proposition to run for city comptroller. He shared his feelings of ambivalence toward the partnership he'd been offered back in Houston. He spoke honestly about his confusion over everything.

Kellie said nothing as the words tumbled out of his mouth. He couldn't help but notice the tears in her eyes. At one point he grabbed her hand.

"I feel terrible about the fact that I haven't asked you what you wanted till now." He spoke passionately. "But I've assumed all along I knew what the Lord wanted."

"You've never been the type to assume," she assured him. "I think you've always acted out of practicality, common sense."

"I know, but —" He glanced at the moving truck. Frankie and Julia stood beside it, deeply engaged in conversation with Kenton and Norah. "Look at them." He gestured. "Some people would say they don't have it as good as we do."

Kellie's brow wrinkled as she responded. "Financially, you mean?"

Nathan shook his head. "Not just that. We have our education. We also have amazing jobs with plenty of advancement opportunities. We have a wonderful home in a great city and plenty of money in the bank so we don't have to live paycheck to paycheck."

"What are you saying, Nathan?" Kellie's eyes remained moist.

"I'm saying that maybe, just maybe, I've placed my security in the wrong things. Maybe the Lord wants to free us up — to give us reason to live in faith." His thoughts flowed from the tip of his tongue without constraint. "Maybe He wants us to let go of some of our material possessions and live a simpler life. That's what I'm saying."

Even as the words were spoken, Nathan felt as if a huge weight had been lifted from his shoulders. All of his adult life he'd had to prove himself. Jockeying for a better position at the firm, investing in a better place to live, setting aside money into bigger, better types of accounts.

And for what?

He bit his lip and waited for Kellie's response. He knew she had grown accustomed to nice things — a modern home and frequent gifts. He also knew she'd grown to appreciate and understand their fast-paced lifestyle with its perks. And yet she seemed to thrive here, in Greenvine.

Which would she choose, if given the opportunity?

Kellie choked back tears and fought for words. For days she had prayed Nathan would come to this decision, but now that the Lord had answered her prayers, she could hardly believe the words coming from her husband's lips or the passion that seemed to drive them.

She wrapped her arms around his neck and leaned into his chest. "N–Nathan."

"I can't tell if you're happy or sad." He pulled back to look into her eyes.

She shook her head. "I'm happy, baby. You don't know how happy."

A look of relief flooded his face. "Why didn't you say something before now?" he asked. "You let me go on and on, setting my sights on life in the city. I must've sounded like an idiot."

"No," she whispered, "I told you last night — I'd follow you to the ends of the earth. If you'd said we needed to move to Alaska, I would have gone." She gave him a shy smile. "At least I'd like to *think* I would have. But the truth of the matter is, my heart is here." She gestured to the worn-down little house. "I love this place. I know it doesn't make much sense, but I do. And I can see us here, years from now, with children of our own."

"Really?" He looked at her with some degree of curiosity. "You wouldn't miss living in a nicer place?"

"Nathan, look around you." She gestured to the property, their friends, her parents. "This *is* a nicer place. And I don't need a fast-paced life or lots of money to enjoy myself. I've had the time of my life these last few months. Less is more, you know?"

He nodded as his gaze traveled from person to person. "Yes." He sighed. "I'm just relieved to hear you say it out loud. I've been trying not to let myself get caught up in the lifestyle these people enjoy, but I want to. I want what they have."

She put her hand to her stomach and prepared to speak the words she'd been holding back for days. "Since you've said that, there's something I need to tell you." She took a deep breath and plowed ahead. "Nathan, you're going to have to build on an extra room." She swallowed hard before adding, "A nursery."

"W–what? W–when?"

"In about seven and a half months." Kellie couldn't hold back the grin as his eyes widened. "I've known for a while now."

"You're kidding." He shook his head and stared at her as if they were strangers. Suddenly light dawned in his eyes. "That's why you were so sick this morning."

Kellie nodded but said nothing.

"Why didn't you tell me? I can't believe you didn't say anything."

She shrugged. "I knew your decision to stay or to go would be swayed by knowing. I needed you to make a decision based on your heart, not on our circumstances."

He continued to shake his head, clearly unable to formulate words. "I don't believe it." The edges of his lips curled up. "I'm going to be a dad." Fear registered. "Not that I have any clue how to do that."

"You'll learn." Kellie gestured in Frankie's direction. "And he'll help you, I'm sure. He's an awesome father."

"He is." Nathan looked at her with eyes

filled with love. "And you're going to be the best mother in the world."

Kellie smiled. "If I'm half as good as Julia, I'll be doing well. It's going to be quite a change from what I'm used to, but I can't wait." Her heart swelled with joy, and she and Nathan crossed the yard, hand in hand.

Nathan shook his head, overcome by Kellie's revelation. No wonder she'd acted so emotional these past few days. No wonder she didn't want to settle back into her old life at the condo. Her perceptions had changed because her situation had changed.

Kellie interrupted his thoughts with her next question. "Speaking of not waiting — what should we do with the condo?"

He shrugged. "Sell it? Rent it out? Doesn't matter. It's not as if we'll be needing it anymore."

She nodded. "If we sold it, we could use the money to fix up this house." They turned to face the little wood-framed home together, hand in hand.

"Good point." He nodded in agreement.

"We've spent a lot of time talking about the future," Kellie continued. "But the future is here. Now. This is what we've talked and prayed about. It's happening right in front of us."

Nathan wrapped her in his arms and gave way to the lump in his throat. The tears that followed came from a place he'd not visited in quite some time.

The future is now.

And no time like the present to enjoy it.

EPILOGUE

Fall blew into Greenvine, and with it came a host of changes. None was more wonderful than those in Nathan and Kellie's lovely renovated home tucked away beneath the pine trees. Inside that place love had grown, doubts had dissipated, and a new little bundle of joy now brought a sense of wonder and awe. By the time fall shifted into early winter, a new season of hope had truly begun.

Nathan contemplated these things as he made his way down the hallway toward the baby's room.

"Honey, are you ready?" He popped his head in the door of the nursery to find Kellie changing their son's diaper.

"Almost." She finished the process, then swept baby Logan into her arms. As she cradled him against her shoulder, Nathan thought his heart would leap from his chest.

"That's the most amazing picture I've ever seen."

"What?" Kellie looked at him curiously.

"You and Logan. Together. Like that." He felt the sting of tears. "It's perfect." An idea struck him. "Don't move. I'll be right back."

He raced into the master bedroom and pulled out his new camera. Entering the nursery again, he began snapping photos from every angle. Kellie shook her head as always.

"We have hundreds of pictures of him already."

"So?"

"You're so cute." She walked over to him and placed Logan into his arms. "Would you mind holding him for a few minutes while I put on some powder and lipstick?"

"Of course not." The baby squirmed, and Nathan responded by rocking him back and forth.

"Oh," Kellie added, "and would you go ahead and put his jacket on? It's a little cool out today."

"Sure." Nathan reached into Logan's closet and pulled out the light blue jacket with a bumblebee on the front. They'd purchased it at a local supercenter. Nothing was too good for his son. He slipped the jacket on and held the baby up in the air until he squealed with delight.

"Nathan," Kellie scolded from down the hall. How did she always know?

Nathan made his way out into the living room with Logan in his arms. Once there, he settled down onto the sofa and focused on the baby's face. Soft blond wisps of hair and bright blue eyes seemed only natural on his handsome son. And talk about smart! Not yet two months old and already holding his head up and smiling. It wouldn't be long before he'd be scooting all over the place.

Kellie came back out into the living room. She paused for a glimpse in the hall mirror and fussed with her hair. "I look awful," she said.

"You're gorgeous," he said and meant it. Sure, she'd changed a little over the past year, but those changes had transitioned her into the woman of loveliness who stood before him now. He wouldn't change a thing — about her or the wonderful life they now shared.

As they stood to leave, Nathan took a good, long look around his house. No longer the run-down home it had once been, the place now testified to the wonders of transformation.

Then again, so did he.

"Ready?" Kellie lifted the baby from his arms. "We have a big evening ahead of us. And I know my mother could use my help setting up."

"I'm ready." He helped her gather up the baby's things, and they walked to the car together. No longer a sports car but a practical SUV sat in the driveway. Logan's car seat had its place of honor in the backseat.

They pulled the car out onto the highway, chatting all the way. Kellie told Nathan about her new part-time job at the brokerage house in nearby Brenham. She shared her joy at how well Logan seemed to have adapted to a few hours a day at Julia's house.

Nathan shared his excitement over his work for the people of Greenvine. Then they talked about tonight's big plans at her parents' home.

In short, they talked about today.

"You want to know something funny?" Nathan asked as they pulled into the center of town.

"What's that?"

He smiled as he reflected on what he would say. "Might sound a little cheesy, but I always thought money could buy love."

"What?" She giggled. "Really?"

He nodded. "Well, in a manner of speaking. I thought that if we had the right combination of things — great jobs, a high-end home, expensive trips — happiness would follow." He glanced back at the sleeping child in the backseat. "But I was wrong."

"Funny how different we are from the people we were just a year and a half ago," Kellie said. "But I wouldn't change a thing. Would you?"

"Nope." He reached to give her hand a squeeze. "I wouldn't change a thing."

Kellie's heart leaped for joy as they pulled into her parents' driveway. Her father stood on the front porch, fussing with the screen door. He waved, then joined them at the car.

"Daddy, you shouldn't be outside. It's chilly out here," Kellie scolded.

He shrugged. "That screen door is getting rusty. Just cleaning the hinges." He gave her a wink. "It's one of the perks of retirement. I can fuss around the house all day. Drive your mother crazy."

Kellie laughed.

Her father's eyes sparkled as he looked into the backseat. "How's that grandson of mine?"

"As feisty as ever." Kellie lifted Logan

from his car seat and placed him into his grandfather's outstretched arms. "And very anxious to see his grandpa."

"He's a handsome fellow." Her father ran his fingers through the baby's curls.

"Yes, he is," Kellie agreed. Logan was a dead ringer for Nathan. How could she think otherwise?

They entered the house with hearts full. Kellie headed straight to the kitchen to help her mother. They still had a couple of hours before guests would arrive for tonight's festivities but decided to go ahead and set the table. They shifted back and forth from kitchen to dining room, carrying food, paper plates, and silverware. Kellie set up the punch bowl and checked the refrigerator to make sure she had the necessary ingredients for later.

They finished up as quickly as they could, but when all was said and done, her mother stood back and surveyed the dining room with a look of concern on her face.

"What's wrong, Mom?"

Her mother shook her head. "I feel as if I'm forgetting something. Wish I could remember what it was." She disappeared back into the kitchen. Moments later, Kellie heard a gasp and ran to her mother's side.

"What is it?"

"I just remembered!" Her mother's face lit up. "Mrs. Dennison is bringing the wedding cake, and I wanted to use that lovely old tray my grandmother passed down to me. I thought it would be perfect for your big night!"

Kellie smiled at her mother's thoughtfulness. "Sounds great! Where is it?"

Her mother bit her lip and stood in silence a moment before answering. "Oh, I remember now. I packed it away in a box with some old family heirlooms years ago. It's at the top of the closet in your old room." She looked at Kellie with renewed excitement. "I haven't had a chance to use it for years. It seems kind of silly to have it sitting in a closet when I could be using it. Would you mind getting it for me, honey?"

"Of course not. I'd be happy to."

Kellie passed through the living room, where she would soon renew her vows, gave all three of her men kisses on their foreheads and kept going until she arrived in her old bedroom. Once inside, the usual warm memories surfaced. Her mother had changed little in this room throughout the years, and she loved coming in here to reminisce.

The same twin bed with ruffled floral bedspread sat underneath the window. A worn teddy bear leaned against the pillows. The chest of drawers that had once held her personal belongings stood in its place on the far left wall. Her little study desk and chair sat to her right. A colorful paint-by-numbers rendition of a horse still clung to the wall over the desk. It was every bit as charming as it had ever been, and she drank in the joy it brought.

"Whatcha doin' in here?"

Kellie turned as she heard her husband's voice. "Oh! You scared me."

"Sorry about that." He walked over to her and wrapped his arms around her. "That's the last thing I wanted to do." He looked at her intently. "What are you doing? Thinking of backing out? Leaving me at the altar?"

She giggled. "I came in here to get something for my mother and got lost in my usual little-girl memories."

"I understand. That's the same feeling I get when we're together in our little house with Logan tucked away in bed. I think they call that *contentment*."

"Yes." Kellie leaned her head against his shoulder, overcome by feelings of joy and peace. "I don't know when I've ever been this content. What about you?"

"I" — his voice broke — "I sometimes wonder what we ever did to deserve all the

Lord has done for us. He's been awfully good to us."

"And you've been so good to me." Kellie looked up, her eyes filling with tears. "You've sacrificed so much over the past year. You didn't have to, but you did. And I love you so much for it. You'll never know how much."

Nathan pressed tiny kisses into her hair. "It doesn't feel like sacrifice now. Just feels good. Right. Like this room."

Kellie looked around, her heart full. "I feel as if I'm all grown up now. I'm not a little girl anymore. And yet having the baby makes me feel . . . reminiscent."

"Nothing wrong with that."

They stood in silence for a moment. Logan let out a cry from the living room, and Kellie looked up with a shrug. "I'd better go see about him."

"I'll take care of it," Nathan said. "You go back to what you were doing for your mom."

"Sure?"

He gave her a warm kiss, then headed out into the hallway.

Kellie walked toward the closet. It still had that funny smell she remembered so well from childhood. She turned on the light and looked around, trying to figure out where the box might be. "Aha." There. Just above her to the left.

She pulled the chair into the closet and climbed up on it to have a closer look. The box proved to be heavier than she'd remembered. She struggled with it but finally freed it from its place.

She set the box on the bed and opened it with great care, knowing the value of the things it contained. How many times had she and her mother looked through this box during her childhood? How many times had she and her sister snuck into the closet for another peek at the goodies inside?

One by one, Kellie lifted out the items: an oval photograph of her great-grandmother, a carefully wrapped gravy bowl, and several chipped and worn figurines.

After Kellie lifted out the large tray, her hand hit upon another item wrapped in newspaper. Funny, but this one didn't ring a bell. She examined the newspaper for clues. The stories appeared to be from another era, but not her grandmother's time. More like —

More like my time.

Her heart filled with joy as revelation hit. "Oh, Lord. Is this what I think it is?"

Gingerly she pulled back the layers of paper. Kellie gasped as the small pink piggy bank revealed itself. She clutched it to her chest, and a lump rose in her throat. The memories came back at once. She'd taken the piggy bank, stuffed full of coins, and hidden it away so she wouldn't be tempted to spend the money. She'd tucked it away in a safe place, knowing she might need it in the future.

This is the future.

With the tray in one hand and the piggy bank in the other, she practically sprinted back into the kitchen. She approached her mother with tears in her eyes.

"Thanks so much, honey." Her mother reached to take the tray, then gave her an odd look. "W–what's happened? Is everything okay?"

"Yes." Kellie held out the piggy bank and bounced up and down with excitement.

Her mother clamped her hand over her mouth and shook her head, clearly not believing her eyes. "Kellie, I don't believe it."

"I'm not sure I do either." Kellie clutched the familiar little pig in her hands and smiled. "But there's got to be some reason why the Lord dropped it in my lap, don't you think?"

"I suppose you'll have to ask Him."

At that moment, Nathan walked into the kitchen, mouth stuffed full of cheese and crackers. "Ask who? What?"

Kellie smiled and held up the piggy bank.

"What's that?" He popped another cracker in his mouth.

"My old piggy bank," she responded. "At least it used to be mine. Years ago." She beamed with delight. "I put a lot of time and effort into saving for the future with this little guy."

"Really?" Nathan's eyes lit up. "So you're saying there's quite a nest egg in there? Enough for a second honeymoon?"

She nodded. "Well, quite a little nest egg for an eight-year-old. That's how old I was when I lost him."

Nathan's eyes grew large. "And you just found it now?"

"I did." She grinned. "Just now."

"Wow." He drew near and looked at her intently. "So what are you going to do with all that money?"

"That's a good question." Kellie stared at the little bank with renewed interest. "I worked for years to fill him up."

She had invested all her excess change — had even done without some of the luxuries her sister had enjoyed, all for the future.

This is the future.

The words rang out in her spirit once again, and Kellie knew immediately what she must do. She reached into a nearby drawer and pulled out a hammer. With one fell swoop, she split the little piggy in two. Coins scattered across the kitchen counter, and a few even rolled off onto the floor. She scooped every last one up into her hands and let out an animated holler.

The noise drew her father and Logan in from the next room. Her entire family stood in shocked silence, watching her every move.

"Kellie?" Nathan stared at her in amazement. "What are you doing?"

She looked up into her husband's concerned eyes and laughed. "I'm going to invest in something we can all use — here and now."

"And what would that be?" He took her in his arms and planted happy kisses on her forehead.

She looked up with the most serious face she could muster. "I figure there's a good twenty dollars here."

"Right. So — ?"

"So," she looked up at him, joy spilling over. "Twenty dollars might not take us to Europe. I'm not sure it would even put enough gas in our tank to get to Houston. But it's probably about the right amount to take us all out for banana splits."

"What?" Her mother looked stunned.

"You don't mean now, do you? We have people coming over in a couple of hours to watch you renew your vows."

Kellie looked at her watch. "In that amount of time we could swallow down enough ice cream to give us all stomach-aches." She scraped the coins into her purse with the rest of her family looking on.

"But — it's chilly outside. Who eats ice cream when it's chilly out?" Her mother tried to argue, but Kellie put up a hand and stopped her midstream.

"I do."

They continued to stare, and Kellie erupted in laughter. No doubt they thought she'd lost her mind. But she didn't care. She'd been set free, liberated.

"I won't take no for an answer," she said. "And don't you worry about getting back on time. I'm the queen of quick, remember? I won't be late for my own ceremony!"

Her mother nodded, her forehead etched with wrinkles. "I — I remember."

"Well, then, what's keeping us? Let's shake this place!"

The room came alive with activity as everyone darted this way and that to collect their belongings. Her father took the baby, and her mother scurried off into the master bedroom to retrieve a warm sweater. Nathan wrapped her in his arms and pressed one last kiss in her hair. "It's not exactly Europe," he whispered.

A girlish giggle rose up as Kellie gave her response. "Aw, who cares? I hear Europe is *highly* overrated, anyway." She grabbed her purse, now heavy with coins, and looked up into her husband's sparkling eyes. He nodded his approval, and together they sprinted toward the car.

Dear Reader,

Welcome to a collection of faith-based love stories set in the place I know best — south Texas! I was born and raised in this great state and have driven nearly every road mentioned in these three romantic tales. And what fun, to have a book titled Texas Weddings. After all, I have four daughters in their twenties, and we've been in wedding-planning mode for the past several years.

A Class of Her Own was my first novel, written in 2001. I could relate to Laura Chapman (the heroine) in so many ways. Her desire to go back to college in her mid-to-late forties was a passion I shared. Best of all, I got to plan Laura's "mid-life" wedding. What a blast!

A Chorus of One holds a very special place in my heart. My two oldest daughters got engaged within weeks of each other in 2003, and their weddings were only five months apart in 2004! We were in over our heads as I crafted this story about Jessica Chapman, who longed for a Mediterranean-themed wedding extravaganza. All of my daughters are very musical (and all have been involved in musical theater and/or opera), so placing Jessica's wedding "on the state" came naturally.

Banking on Love is an "after the wedding" love story. Why did I choose to write a love story about married people? Because I'm always telling my girls, "You're not just planning for a *day;* you're planning for a *life.*" In this tale about a young married couple facing the challenges of post-wedding life, I was able to do delve into issues that many contemporary newlyweds deal with and give a few tips about how to keep romance alive along the way!

Happy reading!
Janice Thompson